Better Dead

BETTER DEAD

Anthea Cohen

Constable • London

Constable & Robinson Ltd
3 The Lanchesters
162 Fulham Palace Road
London W6 9ER
www.constablerobinson.com

First published in the UK by Constable,
an imprint of Constable & Robinson Ltd 2005

A copy of the British Library Cataloguing in Publication
Data is available from the British Library.

ISBN 1-84529-045-3

Printed and bound in the EU

Chapter One

Amy was her usual boring self during tea. Agnes sighed and was about to get up and take the tea things to the kitchen when she noticed a thin, coloured folder had fallen to the floor. She picked it up: pictures of rather lovely country houses. Agnes thought it was a 'Houses for Sale' list but then she noticed that the first page was headed, in red, 'Take a Break'. Each of the dozen or so houses, which featured one to a page, looked peaceful and inviting. It was the final illustration which interested Agnes . . . She folded the page back and began to read the particulars. The place offered for 'Take a Break' was familiar to Agnes: Brighstone Manor, a very pretty manor house on the Isle of Wight, where Agnes had lived for some time. The actual manor house she hardly knew, she only recognized it because she had motored past once or twice when she had lived there. Actually, she had lived on the Solent side of the Island. The village of Brighstone where the pictured house was situated was on the other side of the Island, a long way away according to people who lived in Ryde or Seaview or Bembridge. Brighstone was miles! That fact had always amused Agnes.

'The Island . . .' Agnes smiled to herself as she looked at the pleasant house. When anyone mentioned 'the Island' instead of the Isle of Wight, it always reminded her of Jane Austen: one of her characters always referred to it as 'the Island' as if no other island existed. The manor house was now a hotel. The terms and particulars were all written below the picture – golf course, swimming pool, a very

5

comprehensive gym, and pleasant company. Agnes smiled again at that claim. How, she wondered, did they know that the company would be pleasant? Anyway, it would be nice to explore the Island again, visit old haunts, revive old memories – some happy, some sad; visit old friends perhaps.

Agnes cleared away the tea things and washed up, then took Polly for a short walk. When she got back, her mind was made up. A week away would be a change, a complete change of people and surroundings. She looked up the number and telephoned Brighstone Manor and booked in for a week, starting on Wednesday – that was in three days' time. She felt quite thrilled at the thought of getting away. Agnes gave Polly her evening meal. She had asked if they allowed pets and the man on the telephone had been charming.

'Yes, certainly we make dogs welcome, madam, though I am sure you will understand not in the dining room. We can supply a daily meal for your dog according to your instruction.'

This reply had pleased her. Many hotels did not allow dogs. She turned to Polly, who was now busy pushing her feeding bowl around the kitchen,

'We are going to the Isle of Wight, Polly – new walks, new smells, new walkies!' Polly looked up from her empty bowl, perhaps wondering if the long, cheerful sentence meant more food. Then, realizing it didn't, she wagged her tail furiously and went off into the sitting room to find her favourite squeaky toy. Agnes did not feel guilty about asking Amy to look after the house and animals – there were fewer now and, anyway, it would be a way in which Amy could thank her for all she had done for her brother, Robert.

Amy looked desolated when Agnes said she was going away for a week. She offered to look after Polly and looked more devastated when Agnes said Polly was coming with her.

Agnes found herself getting quite excited as she packed

a suitcase for the week away. Several pairs of slacks and tops – it was June and the weather, as always, could be variable. Two reasonably smart dresses to wear to dinner in the restaurant, her very favourite pale green linen suit in case she went out to lunch. She grimaced to herself at these thoughts. She had made few friends during her time on the Island and who did she think would be likely to ask her out to lunch or wish to dine with her? No, she would just not worry about company, but go and renew some of her old memories. Maybe swim, or play golf – she would have to hire the clubs but according to the brochure this would present no difficulty. Golf could be a solitary pastime and being alone was never a worry to Agnes. She liked her own company and found people more irritating than silence. One or two friends perhaps might remember her.

Agnes zipped up her case, then packed a small one for Polly: her food dish, her favourite squeaky toy, a box of Bonio biscuits, several cans and trays of dog food in case she should take a dislike to her usual hard tack, a box of which was also included in 'Polly's luggage'. Her bed and blanket could go in the back of the Porsche – and a bottle of water and bowl. This Agnes always carried wherever she was going.

Agnes found the crossing on the car ferry much the same as when she lived on the Island. The only difference was that there were far more large lorries and articulated carriers, carrying food and supplies to the supermarkets that had no doubt increased in number since her own ferry trips. Marks and Spencer, Tesco, Somerfield – the enormous vehicles dwarfed her Porsche. She locked the car, having checked, as she always did, that Polly had water to drink and that one of the windows was open a fraction. She did not like abandoning Polly but it was advised that you left your car during the crossing. She made her way up to the lounge and bought herself a cup of coffee. Sitting, looking around at the rather modern set-up, she found herself hoping that the Island had not changed too much, become too commercialized, gleaming, shining and up to date. Its slowness, its 'take your time' attitude, she had loved – no rush, no hurry. Perhaps it had altered. Brighstone Manor, at least in the brochure, had looked like part of the old Island. But perhaps she was wrong to believe that. They drew nearer and she went back to her car.

As she watched the Island grow closer, Agnes was reminded of her husband. Once when they had been coming back from London, or somewhere abroad, she couldn't remember, there had been a sea mist covering the Island, completely cutting it off from view – just the white sea mist.

'You see, I've always said the Island was only a dream. It doesn't exist at all, really, we imagine it!'

Then the Island, her husband's beloved Island, had slowly appeared like a vision. He had put his arm round her shoulders and sighed with – was it mock relief?

'Oh, there it is, it's come back out of the clouds!'

Suddenly Agnes missed him, more than she had for some time. She thought she was getting used to being alone, but at this moment she wasn't so sure.

She drove off the car ferry behind a big, white lorry. When it drew away the scene was at once familiar, even though it was years since she had left. Polly barked at a passing large dog being walked along the path by a woman who glanced into the car. Agnes drove slowly, taking in the houses and streets and remembering past times in her life.

Agnes did not know Brighstone very well, but you could hardly miss Brighstone Manor. The front was impressive, with large sweeping lawns and a wide driveway. The gold of the gravel gleamed in the June sunshine. The equally wide and impressive gates, tall, black-painted and topped with gold paint, opened automatically as Agnes drove her car up to them. They closed silently behind her. As she arrived at the front door, a man in a short white coat came

8

down the six steps and opened her car door with a flourish.

'May I take your luggage, madam, and park your car?'

Agnes got out of the car and Polly jumped out safely on her lead and wagged her tail amiably at the man. He bent and stroked the dog's head.

'A Porsche, madam, a lovely car, my favourite.'

The white-coated man preceded Agnes up the steps with her cases and Agnes wondered if he said the same about all cars, regardless of their make – Rolls, Rover, or whatever happened to arrive at the front door. She fancied he did.

'There is a dog bed and another small case in the car.'

The entrance hall lived up to the ornate gates. A thick red and royal blue carpet covered the whole area. To the right a well-polished counter, with key and letter racks at its back, was manned by a black-suited, white-bloused, middle-aged woman with neat hair and discreet make-up, who handed the book across the desktop for her to sign, earning Agnes's pleasure by leaning over and greeting Polly, who, as always, gave an answering tail wag.

'Oh, a little Jack Russell, one of my favourite breeds – they are such busy little dogs, aren't they?' Agnes nodded, signed her name and address in the book and pushed it back to the receptionist, who read the entry with interest.

'The little dog is allowed everywhere in the hotel except the dining room and we can supply a meal for her if you wish. Dogs are very welcome here – oh, not, I must say, in the swimming pool.'

Agnes laughed, thanked the woman and followed the man in the short white coat up the rather beautiful staircase to her room, which was as well furnished and as pleasant as the hall. The windows looked out on the pool and beautifully kept garden.

Agnes realized that during the time she had lived on the Isle of Wight she must have passed Brighstone Manor a few times, but the place had changed. To the left of the garden the ground rose steeply, the hill covered with trees

9

and tangled bushes. As she looked up to the top of the rise she saw two men walking along. A bicycle passed them so she decided there must be a path or road at the top of the hill. This brought back a vague memory. Hadn't there been an Upper Lane and Lower Lane in Brighstone? She believed so. It would be fun to go out and explore and find new walks for Polly, and for herself. Meanwhile, dinner was at 7.30 p.m.

Agnes began to unpack, hanging up her clothes and putting her toilet things in the en suite bathroom and on her dressing table. She felt her depression fading away a little and for a moment gave a brief thought to Amy Horrocks, who no doubt was missing her. She tried not to feel too guilty and thought she would send her a card.

Dinner was rather disappointing – not the food, which was exceptional, but the fact that only a few people turned up to eat.

'It will be busy later in the week, madam,' the young waitress assured her after Agnes commented on this. Agnes looked at her enquiringly. 'We have a lot of week-end visitors – people come on Friday and stay until Sunday or Monday. Some stay longer.'

Agnes was pleased to hear this. The large dining room was rather dismal with only half a dozen tables occupied. One or two of these people smiled at Agnes when they saw she was alone and she smiled back, but no one attempted to speak to her when they assembled in the lounge where coffee was served. Agnes did not stay long, she wanted to take Polly out and explore round the manor a little. It was still daylight and a warm evening. Polly would have her meal when they returned.

Agnes went up to her room, to be greeted by a delighted Polly; she put on a light coat and snapped on the nylon lead. The receptionist, still on duty, nodded to her as she made her way across the entrance hall towards the front door. Agnes turned out of the gates toward the wild-looking slope upward. It was rough underfoot but one could see it was a well-used path. To her left as she

10

ascended the trees and bushes got thicker, the ground deeply covered with long-dropped leaves. Polly loved it. She was on the lead extended as far as it would go. She dug in the leaves, used the thick layers as a lavatory – Agnes had her bag and scoop with her but had to admit she couldn't use it in this terrain. Up, up she walked until she was out of breath and stopped to have a look around. The slope on her right ran down quite a long way and ended in the main road. She could see traffic going to and fro – a bus came, stopped, some people got out and the bus drove away. Agnes tried to orientate herself and realized this was the road she had motored along to get to her destination.

Polly was still rushing around amongst the fallen leaves – new ground, new smells. Now and again she gave a sharp excited bark, imagining a rabbit or something live and chaseable. Reluctantly she put up with Agnes shortening the lead and turning back. Agnes was pleased with the walk. She would explore it again tomorrow and go further up, but now she was tired, ready to sample the comfortable-looking bed.

When they got back a waitress came out from the dining room carrying a small plate.

'Your dog's dinner, Mrs Turner.' She took the cover off the dish, a mixture of cut-up beef and vegetables.

Agnes was impressed and pleased at the attention. 'Thank you, but I have brought food for Polly.' But Polly had smelled the meat and her tail was going so fast it was almost invisible. She looked from the dish to Agnes, who took the dish from the girl's hand. To her amusement, the girl lent down and patted Polly's head.

'Enjoy,' she said, then to Agnes: 'We will deliver it from the kitchen each evening, Mrs Turner.'

Agnes mounted the stairs carrying the dish. It did smell good – not Polly's usual food, she had to admit, but after all, both were trying to get out of their usual routine. The walk and this doggy meal were a start.

Chapter Two

Agnes spent the next day driving round the Island, revisiting her old haunts: the flat in Ryde where she had lived, the walks she used to take – no Polly in those days – the restaurants where she had taken friends or had been taken by friends to dine or lunch. Most of the people seemed to have left the Island, or she had lost touch with them. Agnes had to admit to herself that she was not good at keeping up with friends. She was not a letter-writing person, or even one who liked telephoning. She enjoyed, however, going to the places she remembered, some of which brought happy, some unhappy, memories.

Agnes lunched at a hotel in Yarmouth, another familiar place to her. She liked and was enjoying her stay at Brighstone Manor but she wished there were a few more guests there, though now the weekend was approaching she hoped there would be more people arriving for a break. On her way back to the manor she decided she would change and go down to the bar, not something she particularly liked to do alone, but she felt like a drink and Polly was allowed in the bar. Maybe there would be other dogs there, but Polly was a friendly soul and normally liked meeting others of her kind. So far, since Agnes had had her, Polly had never started a dog fight.

The bar was small and rather cosy. The counter was a half-circle of highly polished wood with small dishes of nuts and olives and crisps placed at intervals along its surface. Little mats with pictures of the manor were scattered along the counter and on the tables, six of which were placed along the far side of the bar, two chairs at each, angled so that people sitting drinking at the tables could look out on to the flowery part of the garden. Two white-haired women were seated at one of these tables, talking, smiling and sipping – rather to Agnes's surprise – half-pints of beer or cider. A large man in tweeds leant on the bar. With him were two golden retrievers, one asleep, head on paws, the other sitting up with alert eyes fixed on Polly. Agnes led Polly past them without trouble and seated herself at the far end of the half-circle. Another pair walked in, obviously husband and wife, the man white-haired, military-looking, the wife neat, well-dressed. Harrods-looking. She went and sat at a table while the man went to the bar to order drinks. Agnes ordered a glass of white wine, picked up the dinner menu also on the bar, and mentally chose what she would have for her meal. The food so far had been very good. Suddenly Polly sat up and gave a short, sharp bark, tail wagging furiously. The cause – a rather glamorous blonde had come in leading a white poodle. She went up to the bar. The barman leant over, his face smiling.

'Now, you two, no shenanigans in my bar.'

Agnes said, 'Sit, Polly,' and the little dog obeyed at once.

'Sit,' said the glamorous one to her poodle, who took not the slightest bit of notice. The large man in tweeds grinned.

'One word from you and he does as he likes, eh?'

The glamorous one ignored the remark, but at last the poodle gave up, settled under the legs of the stool and stopped barking, looking around with beady black eyes.

Tonight's dinner was delicious and although Agnes ate alone, she enjoyed it. She was no longer used to having dinner at night. Cooking in the evening meant she would miss television programmes she wanted to see, so she had got used to having 'dinner' at midday. The large meal inhibited her sleeping so she determined that she would take Polly for a walk afterwards, up the ascent at the side of the manor which gave the little dog so much enjoyment.

The late evening was warm and the sky still blue. Agnes walked slowly up the incline, Polly's nylon lead let out to its fullest extent to let her nose through the deep layer of fallen leaves, snuffling, occasionally digging and scattering the leaves, busy front paws exposing the sweet-smelling loam underneath. Occasionally a bird would flutter by, making Polly pause in her digging and look up. Agnes continued her walk, going rather further up the incline than she had done before. The path curved a little and she was surprised to find that the ground under her feet became smoother and the path wider and more road-like. She was also surprised to find, just round the bend, a fairly large white-painted house – quite a well-proportioned building, spoiled by a built-on square-shaped garage, doorless and the car parked inside, gleaming red. Agnes wondered whether the owner of the house and car had been instrumental in making the road wider and suitable for the car, taking it down to the main road which she had seen further back. Opposite the house was a slope down, covered with trees and tangled bushes and brambles. The wider road looked boring, so Agnes decided to turn back. She felt tired now and ready for bed. Even Polly walked sedately behind her on the way down. She was nearly back at the entrance to the manor garden when someone walking towards her in the dusk made her jump.

'Nice walk, Mrs Turner? Lovely evening, isn't it?'

Agnes peered into the gloom at the man. At first she didn't recognize him at all, then his face came back to her memory. It was the white-coated porter who had greeted her on her arrival at Brighstone Manor and had parked her car and carried her suitcases, flattering the Porsche.

'Oh, yes, good evening. Very nice walk, thank you.'

He smiled a little, looking sideways at her. He took a long pull at the cigarette he held in his hand, hidden until that moment. Agnes for some reason disliked his manner. She had to sidestep to get past the man. He began to

14

mount the hill, blowing out a long plume of smoke as he did so. There was arrogance in his walk, as if he was aware that Agnes might be watching him.

The manor house – every room lit up and the trees in the front garden festooned with little lights as well – looked impressive. As Agnes entered, the night receptionist, a rather elderly man, came forward and asked if she required anything. This pleased her. She thanked him and said no. She was glad she had come. Already she felt less bored, less depressive. She gave Polly a biscuit and filled her water bowl. Polly went to her bed, taking her biscuit with her. Agnes spread a small blanket that she had brought from home on her own bed, knowing that Polly would leap on to the bed a little later and sleep at Agnes's feet, as she always did.

Agnes had her shower. She sank thankfully into the comfortable bed, looked at her little bedside clock – twenty to eleven, earlier than she normally went to bed. Polly gave a little snore: she was already asleep. In ten minutes, so was Agnes.

The next morning when Agnes arrived in the dining room, she found two more tables occupied, one by the owner of the two retrievers, who had been joined by a woman about his own age, presumably his wife. He waved a hand at Agnes as she passed his table and spoke to the woman with him, probably telling her that Agnes also had a dog with her. Or so Agnes guessed.

After breakfast she went back to her room to fetch Polly. Her idea was to put Polly in the car and take her to new ground, but Polly would have none of it and pulled firmly towards the start of the little hill. Agnes gave way to her as she usually did, not suspecting that this time the now familiar walk was to be a little more interesting and puzzling. Polly made her normal dive for the damp piled leaves, relieved herself and made a great deal of scratching up leaves and earth to scatter around. Agnes felt she had never seen the little dog enjoy a walk so much. Perhaps it was the floor of old leaves, the fall of many autumns never cleared away, just left to rot and turn into the perfect compost, smelly, soft and 'dog perfect'.

Agnes indulged Polly and strolled slowly up the incline, occasionally looking through the trees to the main road where she could see the cars going by, and glancing at the rise to her other side. It was one of these glances that caused her to stop and cross over the path. She could see a corner of a box or some sort of container pushed under a tangle of weeds, almost hidden but not quite. Whoever had hidden it there had not been quite careful enough. Agnes shortened Polly's lead and went to investigate. She had to push through a little growth of brambles and was glad she had put slacks on this morning.

It was not a box, but a briefcase, a fairly old and worn briefcase, scuffed at the corners. The lid was wet either with rain that might have fallen in the night or with the morning dew. Agnes was about to open the two silver catches, still bright and usable by the look of them, then suddenly she realized how stupid she was being. There might be anything in the case – a bomb even, though she had to admit that this was pretty unlikely. Who would leave a bomb where, if it was detonated, it would do so little harm? Even so, she drew away. It might hold drugs, hidden there to be collected. She decided to leave it and perhaps tell someone about it at the hotel later.

Back at the manor she still felt perhaps she was being rather stupid – after all, it was nothing to do with her. She would feel foolish saying that she had found an old brief-case in the bushes. Probably it had been there for ages. Agnes hated the thought of drawing attention to herself over such a trivial matter. She went to her room, changed her slightly snagged slacks for another pair. She was off to Shanklin to have coffee with an old acquaintance she had played Scrabble with when she lived on the Island. The Scrabble friend was a great lover of Jack Russells and had two of her own – a reason for Agnes to renew the rather nebulous contact. When she had telephoned Mrs Robson, she had told her about Polly and a little of her history. Mrs

Robson, in her late seventies or eighty by now, had begged her to come and bring Polly.

'I can't walk much nowadays, Mrs Turner,' she had said. This had made Agnes feel sorry. She had remembered her as lively and sprightly – age could not have been kind to her. This visit was livelier than Agnes had anticipated. Mrs Robson's two dogs were not young but accepted Polly and very soon the three of them were tearing round the back garden of Mrs Robson's bungalow. The garden was securely walled in so there was no risk of the trio escaping. Mrs Robson was severely disabled but could walk round indoors and managed to wheel the coffee out into the garden.

'I've got a wonderful friend who walks the boys daily. It's such a help. She loves them, I think, as much as I do. I'm so lucky, I still play Scrabble – four of us play here once a week,' she smiled.

Agnes left her thinking two things: would she be as cheerful and lively as her friend if she became as disabled? The second thought was about her house. Was the fact that it was so isolated, once she was in it, making her so depressed? Agnes tried to shake the feeling off. Her mind turned to the briefcase. Perhaps she would go and open it after all, if it was still there, see if it contained anything exciting. Something in Agnes at this moment craved some kind of stimulus. She knew and recognized this feeling and feared it. It often came when she was fending off her dreaded depression.

Agnes got back to the manor at about twenty to six, which gave her time for the luxury of a lie-down on her bed with her favourite book of the moment. Polly leapt up beside her. Both fell asleep. When she woke she grabbed her little bedside clock – twenty to seven. A soft knock on her door. Agnes opened it and outside was Polly's dinner. The dog smelled it and began to dance about in anticipation. Agnes put down the small plastic mat she had brought with her and Polly set to, making the snorty, slurping noise she always did when she was enjoying her daily meal.

Agnes had a quick shower and changed into a dress. She stood back from the long mirror to get an 'all-over view'. The dress was a lavender colour, well cut, and it was the first time Agnes had worn it. She was pleased with her reflection. Her figure was good and the new dress showed it off to perfection. Her hair, which as a young nurse had been her despair, was now well cut, showing a few grey hairs, but the treatments and frequency of her visits to the hairdresser had tamed it and now, if it blew about, it fell back into place.

She remembered only too well how she had felt and how she had been when she first started her training: self-esteem nil, shy, retiring, no boyfriends or, come to that, girlfriends either. Agnes always felt she had wasted her youth, but as she looked at herself in the mirror now, she was pleased at what she saw. She left the room, locking the door behind her. Polly would fall asleep after finishing her meal.

As she entered the dining room, she was greeted by a waiter who showed her to her table and handed her the menu with a flourish. Agnes looked around her. There were more people – at least twenty. Some tables had four people, some two. It made the place look more attractive, Agnes thought, but she felt a little embarrassed by the fact that she was the only person seated alone at a table.

Agnes was just consulting the menu when a voice interrupted her. She looked up. It was the man with the two retrievers – she had christened him 'the tweedy man' because of the rough tweed suit he had been wearing in the bar. This evening, however, he looked quite different in a dark suit. He smiled.

'Met you in the bar. Name's Martin, Martin James.'

Agnes smiled back at him and told him her name.

'We wondered, my wife and I, if you would care to join us. It's our fortieth wedding anniversary. It would be nice to add a guest to our little celebration.'

The invitation should be accepted, Agnes felt. It had been so nicely put and the pair looked and sounded as if they really wanted her. The man's wife was smiling and looking towards them.

'Thank you, I would like to join you,' she said. She got up and walked over to the other table.

He introduced his wife – her name was Maureen. He spoke to the waiter who, on Agnes's instructions, had moved her cutlery, napkin and glass to the Jameses' table. His quiet order was obviously for another bottle of champagne for one shortly appeared and was thrust into the ice bucket at the side of the table. Agnes's wineglass was changed by the same waiter for a flute glass, which her host filled. It was a pleasant meal. The conversation was quite interesting – dogs, of course, formed part of it, books and television. The time flew past. The staff, who one could tell knew about the celebration, were particularly attentive. It was nine twenty when Agnes at last excused herself, giving Polly's walk as an excuse.

Upstairs Agnes changed her shoes and put on a light coat. She decided she would not try and solve the mystery of the briefcase tonight: she did not want to spoil her dress, which had received compliments from both Maureen and her husband. Polly had licked her plate clean. Agnes put the plate outside the door, clipped on the lead and set off down the stairs for Polly's night walk. There was a full moon and the night was warm and soft. Agnes smiled to herself as she started up the little hill, which had been mentioned at the table this evening. Martin had made a remark about it.

'You don't have to take a scoop. They can do their business in the leaves and cover it up.'

This had provoked a rather prim remark from Maureen, who had rebuked her husband, tapping him on the hand.

'Not at the dinner table if you don't mind, Martin.'

Martin had apologized and made a little grimace at Agnes.

Agnes was glad she had chosen to have this break; she had needed it. She thought of the case as she passed where it was hidden but made no move towards it. Tomorrow, perhaps, she would investigate. Polly pulled her off to the wooded, leafy side – she had smelled a smell. Agnes let the nylon lead out and stepped into the shadows. She heard light footsteps almost running, maybe from the house at the top of the hill. It was a young girl, a very young girl. Agnes had a good view of her in the moonlight. The girl made straight for the little depression where the briefcase was hidden. Agnes watched. The girl did not even glance her way. After the girl had disappeared into the under-growth, Agnes heard the snap of the clasps of the briefcase. The girl had been wearing what looked like a tracksuit – black trousers with a white strip running down each leg, white trainers, a black top with a white strip across the chest. When she emerged from the bushes, the change was startling. A short, short skirt, black high-heeled shoes with straps round the ankles, a skimpy low-cut white top. The girl had released her hair, which had been tied back in a ponytail and was now loose and fair and frizzy. She crossed the lane up ahead of Agnes and hurried down the lower lane that led to the main road. When she was halfway down, walking pretty quickly in spite of the shoes, Agnes could move and look down at the wood. A man was waiting at what Agnes presumed was the bus stop. She could not make out, even in the moonlight, how old he was – only that he was a good head taller than the girl. They embraced, then almost at once the bus to Newport drew up. One passenger, a woman, got out and made her way back up the road. The girl and man got into the bus and it drove away.

Where had the girl come from? Agnes felt it must be the house at the top of the hill. She walked further, much to Polly's delight. There was a light on in a downstairs room. Upstairs the room over the garage was in darkness, but the window was half open. Was that where the girl had come from? Escaped to meet the boy or man? She looked so

20

young in spite of the clothes – the whole, very seductive outfit had looked out of place. She still looked about thirteen or fourteen. Surely the parents must suspect – it would be so easy to catch her clambering on to the garage roof out of her window and down to the garden. Agnes looked at her watch. It was ten to ten. She turned to go back to the manor. She was haunted as she walked back down the hill by the thought of her own youth, hemmed in on all sides by the nuns who had brought her up. Her mind was split between admiration for the bravery of this young creature, and worry about her stupidity and the danger she was putting herself in. By the time she had reached the hotel she was still undecided. Should she tell – protect this girl? Or let her have the life she wanted? By the time Agnes was ready for bed she had arrived at a decision that she would regret. It was none of her business – she would keep the matter to herself. The girl was not her business. Even so, it was quite a long time before she went to sleep, and even then her dreams were troubled.

Chapter Three

The Brighstone Manor Hotel had a very useful and unusual facility. Way out at the back of the manor, well away from the swimming pool, the putting green, the well-kept lawns and flowerbeds, was a large fenced-off area. The rails surrounding it were painted white and at the entrance was a notice reading 'Pooh Corner'. Rather twee, Agnes had thought when she had seen it on her first morning, but still a very good idea. Agnes was an early riser and was usually up, bathed and dressed by about eight fifteen. Polly, by this time, was ready to 'relieve herself' as the lady receptionist had delicately put it when she had explained the procedure on Agnes's arrival.

Agnes could take Polly down to Pooh Corner, then after the little dog had performed, she could take her back to her room and give her the morning dog biscuit before going down to the dining room to have own breakfast at leisure. On her first morning she had met another 'dog reliever' on the way and wished him a 'Good morning'. He had been wearing his dressing gown and leading a spaniel, but had looked the other way and had not exchanged a greeting. Agnes felt sympathetic towards him when she had later seen him at breakfast with his wife: she appeared to be a lady who certainly would never allow anyone to see her unless she was in her full 'warpaint', hair, make-up, clothes all perfectly present and correct. Agnes liked to be properly dressed before anyone saw her in the morning, but she drew the line at heavy blue eyeshadow, sparkling earrings and shoes with three- or four-inch heels.

This morning she had intended to go and look again at a cottage she had passed yesterday on the lower Brighstone road, but Polly had other ideas as she came out of the hotel's front door and headed to where the Porsche was parked. Polly made for the front gate with great determination – her favourite walk and digging place firmly in her doggy mind. Agnes gave way to her as she normally did, not only for Polly's sake but because the girl and the scene she had witnessed yesterday had added interest to the hill.

Her feelings were still divided about the girl she had watched running down the path towards the road in those perilous heels, running to meet the bus, to adventure, to her boyfriend, man, lover or whoever it was waiting for her. She looked so young, so thrilled, so excited.

Agnes's memory was again thrown back to her own youth. No risks were ever taken, her self-esteem was so low she was sure no one, no one, would ever want to put his arms round her, fall in love with her. Terror always accompanied the idea. She was too ugly, too shy, too awkward. She tried to banish all thoughts of that time. If she dwelled on it, it always brought back the dreaded depression, which would overcome her.

The day was sunny and warm. Polly shared her delight on the end of her extended lead. She was where she wanted to be, where she could chase imaginary small creatures, dig, throw up showers of old shiny, rotting leaves, follow smells galore, new and old. Agnes walked slowly, enjoying her pet's enjoyment, taking in the soft, sweet-smelling air.

When Agnes reached the top of the incline, she looked more closely at the house. There was the window above the garage roof, still open. She could clearly see and understand how the youngster could easily drop the couple of feet from what was presumably her bedroom window on to the garage. The climb down from the roof to the ground would be more hazardous and certainly impossible in a minuscule skirt, fishnet tights, high-heeled chunky shoes and a short, white see-through top that did not cover her midriff. Agnes could not help smiling to herself, rather ruefully. Freedom and danger the young ones craved. Perhaps the girl's parents were strict, older – 'In at nine thirty, no boyfriends.' No wonder the girl kept her rather bizarre clothes hidden away.

Agnes had almost passed the hedge that bordered the front garden and divided it from the lane, when a woman's voice stopped her.

'Excuse me, may I have a word with Polly, your dog? I've seen you go by – she's such a love.'

'How did you know her name was Polly?'

The woman moved along the hedge to the gate, opened it and looked with delight at Polly, bent down and stroked the little dog's head. Agnes stood there, not knowing quite how to handle the situation. Polly had entered the open gate, always ready to have a fuss made of her. Agnes was still outside, holding the end of the extended lead.

The gaze travelled from the dog to Agnes, who was standing outside the gate, trapped, as it were, by the length of nylon leash, Polly dancing on the other end.

'Oh, forgive me, I'm so sorry, do come in. May I offer you a cup of coffee? I was just going to make myself one. My name's Thelma Ryman.' She extended a hand. Agnes took it and came through the gate.

'My name is Agnes, Agnes Turner. Polly's name you already know. Yes, I would like a coffee. Thank you very much.'

Mrs Ryman guided Agnes through a rather small glass and white-painted porch over the front door. She paused and took off her wellingtons and stood them tidily on the tiled floor, then slipped her feet into a pair of soft, brown suede shoes, apologizing at the same time for keeping Agnes waiting. They moved forward, then, into a large hallway. Polly's paws made a clicking noise as she ran over the polished pine floor, then she took a sliding ride on one of the rugs that were dotted about. Both Agnes and Thelma Ryman laughed at this and Polly's lead was shortened a little.

'Do sit down and I'll make the coffee, Mrs Turner.'

She left the room, and Agnes looked around. Large french windows revealed the flowering back garden. The furniture seemed to be rather old-fashioned; the large over-stuffed three-piece suite was covered in chintzy patterned covers, the valances ironed into perfect pleats, the carpet thick and again flowery. The explanation was soon apparent.

Thelma Ryman came back into the room carrying a tray on which were two large steaming cups of coffee. She put the tray down on the coffee table, then gave a little 'Ouch!' and put her hand to her back.

'Edging the lawn is back-breaking work. I don't think I'm going to do that job again – it's too much for my fifty years to take on, Mrs Turner.'

Agnes was amused that her hostess made no secret about her age. The coffee was delicious and Agnes's remark that it was a long time since she had tasted such good coffee seemed to please Mrs Ryman.

Agnes was always surprised how, if you assumed an air of interest and put on what she called 'a listening face', so many people – even on a very short acquaintance – loved to tell others the circumstances of their own life. She was always surprised because it was so unlike her own attitude. She liked to keep her own counsel and rarely, if ever, told even long-standing friends about her youth, her career as a nurse, or any of the happenings in her own life. However, she did not mind listening to other people's disclosures and in this particular case she felt mildly curious about the young girl she had seen in the lane, running away from the house and not only changing her clothes but her way of life as well. During the first cup of coffee, she learned a great deal about the house and some of the people who made up the household, and why and how

25

they came to have moved to the house only recently, why it looked a little old-fashioned.

The property had belonged to Mrs Ryman's mother, but persistent and disabling arthritis had at last made it impossible for her to look after herself without constant help so a year ago she had moved into a nursing home-cum-residential home in Totland, making over the house to her daughter and son-in-law. The coffee was sipped and more of the story unfolded. When a second cup was suggested, Agnes agreed. She really enjoyed good coffee and wanted to hear more of the story.

Mrs Ryman went out to the kitchen with the tray and after a few minutes came back with two more steaming cups and added to the tray a small plate of almond-flavoured thin biscuits, one of Agnes's favourites. The story continued – told with obvious enjoyment and only one 'I do hope I'm not boring you, Mrs Turner?' Agnes assured her hostess that she was very interested and wondered when the moment would arise when she could ask, 'Have you any children, Mrs Ryman?'

More coffee was sipped and more of the story unfolded. Richard, Mrs Ryman's husband, loved his mother-in-law's house – always had – and when she made it over to them he was delighted. It had come at precisely the right time.

'He was so pleased, I can't tell you how pleased.'

Apparently Richard was an accountant, head of his firm, but at sixty was tiring of the inevitable pressures. A slight heart attack had persuaded him to retire and where better than to the Isle of Wight, one of his very favourite places? The Rymans had let their London house furnished and moved into Fairlight, the house that had come to them rather suddenly.

'My husband is golf mad. Almost as soon as we arrived here to live, he joined the Sandown Golf Club, much cheaper than his London club, of course, so he plays about five days a week or, if he doesn't play, he goes there to socialize. I'm glad for him, he's worked hard all his life and deserves time to play and do the things he wants to do; leave work behind him.'

Agnes admired this selfless attitude but could not help asking the question: 'But what about you, Mrs Ryman, don't you miss London, your friends, the theatres, concerts or whatever was of importance to you?'

The question was not answered immediately. There was a little pause, a small intake of breath. Then, as if she were not too sure how to answer: 'Well, I do, Mrs Turner, I do. But there's the garden and – well, I'm sure I will still make friends here, and our London friends will come and stay in the summer anyway. I shall get used to it.'

At last, Agnes was able to slide neatly into the subject she was more interested in.

'And have you any children, Mrs Ryman?'

'Yes, we have two children, a boy of twenty and a girl. Jeremy is not able to decide what he wants to do and is rather a worry. He gave up university before getting his degree and, as he puts it, "took off to have a tour around and see the world". We hear from him occasionally, mostly when he's short of money. We believe he's in India at the moment, but not sure what he's doing – whether he's working, earning any money. I worry about him. His father's not as concerned as I am, says it will do Jeremy a world of good to see new countries, experience new cultures – maybe he's right. He wants to be a painter.'

Mrs Ryman shrugged her shoulders and made a little grimace. Agnes got the feeling that she was not the happiest of women, was at the moment rather friendless and perhaps not getting all the support she needed from her now retired, golf-playing husband. However, Agnes could not suppress her curiosity about the teenage girl of the household.

'And your daughter – is she younger than Jeremy?'

At the mention of her daughter, Mrs Ryman's face lit up: this was something about which she was happy. She smiled widely, sat up straight and pushed back her rather pretty hair, grey and naturally curly.

'Oh, she is younger – fourteen – well, fourteen and three-quarters, as she is always reminding us.'

Agnes smiled, too. The mother's enthusiasm to tell her about her daughter, all about her daughter, made her glance at her wristwatch, but it was a few minutes before she could stem the flow she had started with her question. It was all praise – by the sound of her mother's comments the girl could do no wrong, was not a trouble, never had been. Agnes felt this girl was a very unusual teenager, very unusual indeed – and bore no relation to the girl escaping from her bedroom window and changing from a tracksuit into the very tasty gear Agnes had seen her in.

At last, after a paean of praise about the beloved daughter, her lack of any sort of fault, Agnes managed to say goodbye and thank you to Thelma Ryman. They had, at the end of the meeting, agreed to use Christian names. As she made her way down the hill with Polly, who never tired, and rushed around on the end of her leash, Agnes could not help going over the loving praise from the mother and comparing it with what little she knew about the girl's behaviour.

Apparently, the girl had been unhappy at her boarding school outside London but had said little about it to her parents. All had been revealed when they told her that they were going to move from London to Granny's house in the Isle of Wight, a place she loved.

'It was only then she admitted she didn't like her school, didn't like the nuns who ran it. Dear girl, it didn't affect her schoolwork but then Tracey would think of us, not want to worry us, so kept it all to herself.'

Agnes had listened to Thelma's effusive outpourings with growing disbelief. No one could be that perfect. Why was the girl behaving with such decorum and yet climbing out of her window and meeting a boy, or a man even, on the nights she was able to get away, perhaps to go to a party or a club with him, dressed in a way that Agnes was sure would upset her mother? And did the boy realize she was only fourteen, were they in love, having sex, was she taking drugs?

Thelma had told Agnes that Tracey was now registered at a small private school in Newport. She was doing well, coming home each evening about five thirty, doing her homework, and, according to her mother, making friends, with one of whom she occasionally stayed for the evening, her father going to fetch her rather than let her come on the bus and walk up the hill.

'She's very sensible, wouldn't speak to anyone or let them speak to her. But you cannot be too careful these days, can you, so her father always fetches her from her friend's, even if it is only early evening. She wanted a bike, but I discouraged that, and she made no fuss about it, but then she never does.'

On and on, Agnes had listened to the doting mother talking about her perfect daughter until she had grown a bit bored. She had left with promises to call again, something her curiosity about the runaway girl might encourage her to do. However, at the moment she dismissed it all from her mind and decided to follow her earlier idea and go and look at the little cottage in Brighstone. Would she like to come back to the Island to live, get away from the mainland for a while, live on her own again? First, lunch somewhere, just a light meal. Then back for another look at the cottage.

While Agnes was eating her lunch, she could not help her thoughts straying back to the morning's conversation. Her own part in it had been rather sparse, but she was intrigued to imagine how well the youngster they had been talking about had perfected living two lives – the dutiful, obedient, examination-passing fourteen-year-old child, and the Tracey who dressed like a seventeen-year-old very 'modern miss' and got up to heaven knows what with a boyfriend. Thelma Ryman would certainly find such a thing impossible to believe.

After lunch Agnes drove to the cottage she had seen and rather liked. 'Cottage' was perhaps the wrong word: the place was fairly modern, perhaps built fifty years ago. The front lawn was large and beautifully manicured – bordered with pansies, a mimosa in one corner in full yellow feathery bloom. The garden was surrounded by trees which gave a deceptive feeling of isolation. Actually the next and rather similar house was quite close, but completely hidden by the trees. Agnes liked the slightly suburban feel this gave – that, and the feeling of being on the Island again was tempting.

'Hello, Mrs Turner. Thinking of joining us on our little Island? Pretty house, isn't it? Desirable Residence, eh?'

Agnes swung round, really startled. She certainly had not heard anyone approaching. For a moment she did not recognize the person who had spoken, then she remembered: it was the man who had parked her car for her when she had first arrived at Brighstone Manor. She had not liked his manner then and she did not like it now. He had a peculiar smirk shaping his rather red lips. He looked as if he was wearing lipstick. He motioned with his hand towards the noticeboard at the gate which named the estate agent in Newport and bore the words 'For Sale' in large red letters.

'I reckon it will soon sell, don't you? If you want it you better . . .' he paused, 'get a move on.'

Agnes cut him short, furious at his familiar, chatty manner. She did not even know the man's name nor had she any wish to know it. She moved towards him.

'Thank you for your advice. I don't know why you offer it, I am certainly not in need of it.'

All the remark did was make the man's smirk become a little more pronounced. Agnes got into the Porsche. She had intended to give Polly a little walk but decided she would rather be as far away from this man as possible. His insolent manner irritated her.

'Who did he think he was? Dreadful little man!' This to Polly as she drove away from the cottage, somewhat faster than she normally did.

A note was waiting for her at the manor from Thelma

Ryman asking her to dinner the following evening. Agnes was rather pleased. She hoped she would meet 'the perfect daughter' and find out how the girl managed to fool her parents into thinking she was safely in bed when she was out with a boy at a club, or at a party of some kind. Agnes's feelings were still divided between admiration and disquiet. What hazards might Tracey be heading for? Drugs, alcohol, sex, a mass of problems she could not possibly cope with at her tender age. Or was it better to jump in at the deep end and learn to handle such things?

Agnes telephoned and accepted the invitation, rather looking forward to it. She had extended her booking at Brighstone Manor by another week: the depression she had been feeling was withdrawing. Agnes wished sometimes she did not know herself so well, wished she did not fear her own moods, recognize at the very onset what was going to overcome her. New people, new friends, always seemed to help.

Chapter Four

Next day she went to the estate agent to learn more about Brook Cottage, the house which, in her opinion, was not a cottage at all. If she did decide to move there she would certainly change the name. The estate agent, Anthony Timms of Timms and Buxton, named a price that Agnes could well afford. Indeed she would make money on the deal – houses on the Island were a good deal cheaper than the mainland. She made an appointment to look over the property the next day with the agent. He warned her that great interest had been shown in Brook Cottage but Agnes, no novice in buying and selling property, was well aware that most estate agents sing that particular song. On the way back she passed the cottage again, just to look at it. This time she saw no sign of the smirking man, but when she drove into Brighstone Manor he was just getting into a Rover 75 – to park it, she supposed – so she was treated again to a rather familiar wave. She did not return it and parked her car herself. Polly and she walked round to the front drive and up the steps into the hall without even looking in his direction again.

After a peaceful rest on her bed with Polly beside her, Agnes decided to walk up the hill to the white house for her dinner date. She would not take Polly but would settle her down in her bed at the manor. Polly did not mind being left as long as she had been fed and walked. She was, thankfully, not a dog who barked constantly when alone, which Jack Russells are inclined to do. Agnes left about an inch of window open in the room and locked the bedroom door, leaving the Do Not Disturb sign on display so Polly could sleep her way through the couple of hours or so she would be away.

She quite enjoyed the walk from the manor up to the house. The air was still and warm, untainted by the smell of traffic even though the main road was fairly close. At last she reached the house, opened the now slightly familiar gate, walked up the path alongside Thelma's back-breaking lawn edging and rang the doorbell. Steps sounded inside, crossing the pine floor of the hall, and a man's voice called, 'I'll get it.' The door opened and a tall, rather plump man greeted her:

'Hello! Do come in – I'm Richard Ryman. You are Mrs Turner, that's right, isn't it? Anthea Turner?'

'Agnes, Agnes Turner – it's easy to get wrong.'

He took the light coat which Agnes had shrugged off her shoulders and handed to him. They went through the hall into the sitting room where Thelma Ryman was just emerging from what Agnes guessed might be the kitchen regions, but then decided she was wrong. When she had drunk coffee with Thelma Ryman the kitchen region was not in that direction, it was through a door further down the room. Mrs Ryman, Thelma, had perhaps come from upstairs and Agnes wondered if she had arrived a little too early for her hosts. In the next minute she knew this was not the case. It was quite a different reason.

'Oh, Agnes, sorry I was not here to greet you. Actually I was upstairs trying to persuade our daughter to come and have dinner with us.'

Agnes smiled and tried to eliminate the anxious feeling she could detect between husband and wife.

'Oh, perhaps she doesn't like meeting new guests?'

Both Richard and Thelma shook their heads in unison.

'Oh, no, it's nothing like that, Mrs Turner – Agnes,' Richard reassured her.

Thelma was equally anxious to explain that this was not the case at all. 'It's eating she objects to. She thinks she is too fat. She is a little plump – well, slightly – but not

33

enough to make her stop eating. It's not that awful anorexia, she's just a little vain. You know how girls are.'

At that moment the door opened and in walked Tracey. Agnes was about to say, 'Has she seen a doctor?' She hastily bit the question back, too intimate, and she did not want the girl to hear her asking such a question about her.

The girl who entered the room was, indeed, the girl Agnes had seen changing her clothes and then running down the dangerous incline to meet her boyfriend, climbing on to the bus bound, presumably, for Newport, or to take her and the boy to goodness know where. Yes, certainly it was the same girl, but so changed. It was as if she had assumed another role in a play. When her mother introduced her she looked at Agnes with a polite lack of interest. She smiled a rather tight smile then walked into the room and sat down. Her dress, her hair, her completely clean, shining face, most of all her manner, could be most aptly described as demure.

'Drinks, darling,' Thelma gently reminded her husband. He jumped up quickly. Agnes chose a gin and tonic with lemon and ice; his wife chose the same. On the coffee table were some small, attractive glass dishes, one holding olives, another nuts, and a wooden shovel-shaped container holding a selection of crisps. Richard poured himself a generous whisky and added a dash – only a dash – of soda water. As he was about to sit down, putting his glass on the table, his daughter spoke, her voice rather husky, the remark accompanied by a sweet smile, a slightly innocent smile, Agnes could not help thinking to herself.

'No one asked me what I would like to drink.'

Her father straightened up at once, apologetic. 'Oh, sorry, Tracey darling, I didn't mean to forget you. What would you like, an orange juice?'

Tracey shook her head and made a little grimace. 'Daddy, may I have a glass of white wine, please? I'm sick of just having soft drinks all the time.'

Agnes watched the little play of reactions between her

34

parents. They hesitated, looked at each other, then her father came to a decision, shrugging shoulders.

'Oh, well, as it's a special occasion, welcoming our new friend Mrs Turner, perhaps a glass of wine could be allowed, don't you agree, dear?'

His wife nodded with – Agnes felt – a certain amount of reluctance. Richard Ryman left the room and made towards the kitchen where the wine was probably chilling in the refrigerator. Agnes heard him speaking in the kitchen and concluded there must be someone cooking the meal. Thelma had not gone out to see if the dinner was progressing, which explained why she could sit and sip her drink with complete relaxation.

'We don't allow this normally, Agnes, but just this once and only one glass, darling.'

'Oh, Mummy, you are so old-fashioned. Everyone drinks wine when they are fifteen, everyone. Don't make a pro-duction of it.'

'I may be out of touch, Tracey, but I think fourteen is a little early to start alcoholic drinking – don't you agree with me, Agnes? I'm sure you do!'

Agnes did her best to be non-committal and shook her head, not wanting to get involved in the question.

'Oh, I really could not give an opinion, Thelma. I have no children of my own, but I can only say that young people today seem to be very much more advanced than in my day. Right or wrong, I couldn't say.'

Agnes looked towards Tracey, who gave her a warm smile as if she felt Agnes was on her side. She took the glass from her father and drank some as if she was well used to wine. Probably she was, Agnes thought. Maybe she should pretend the drink was a little less palatable . . . even as the thought came into her head, Agnes realized she was almost automatically putting herself on the girl's side.

'Mum tells me you have a dear little dog called Polly, Mrs Turner?'

Agnes told her all about Polly's rescue and her life at the

Sanctuary with the other dogs, and both Tracey's parents looked pleased that their guest and their daughter appeared to be getting on so well together. Conversation became general and suddenly an aproned woman appeared to say that dinner was ready.

'Oh, thank you, Mrs Morton, thank you.'

They all moved into the dining room. Although it was not yet dark, the lamps had been put on in various parts of the sitting room and dining room. The amber shades gave the rooms a cosy, comfortable glow that was pleasing – made the rooms look larger.

'Do you like it here better than being in London?' Agnes said as they were seating themselves round the dining-room table.

Tracey answered with enthusiasm: 'Oh, tons better, Mrs Turner. I hated school up there – I was a full boarder. Here I get home every day which is nice, and they are just ordinary teachers. In London they were all nuns. They all smelled so fruity, you know, the nuns did.'

'Tracey, that will do. You shouldn't speak about the nuns like that.'

Tracey's father looked at her, a slight frown on his forehead, but in a quick aside to Agnes he added: 'They did smell a bit fruity, actually,' and he smiled. 'Fusty, you know.'

'Richard, behave yourself and don't encourage her,' Thelma said.

He looked at Agnes and winked, and began to serve the meal, carving with expertise.

The food was excellent. The cook seemed to have taken herself off. There were no more sounds from the kitchen and they waited on themselves. At ten to ten Agnes said she must go back to the manor, using Polly as an excuse for leaving.

'She's very good about being left on her own, but she's in a strange place, not quite her usual surroundings. She might just start to bark and annoy the other guests.'

36

'I'll run you back, it's quite a walk down the hill and round to the manor, and it's dark.'

Agnes thought her host had consumed far too much booze to drive, but he was persistent and went out to back the car into the road. His wife agreed.

'Richard's right. I wouldn't like you to walk home. There are no lights on the hill. Suppose there was someone lurking about? Richard's quite right to drive.'

'It's very kind of him, but I fully expected to walk back – after all, it's only a short distance. I promise you there is no need.'

Richard Ryman put his head round the front door, his red face smiling. The car, lights full on, stood outside the gate, the engine running.

'Your carriage awaits, madam.'

Thelma switched on the light over the front door which illuminated the garden path. She kissed Agnes goodnight. 'You must come again soon,' she said.

In spite of her misgivings, Agnes was driven quite safely back to the hotel and watched while Richard turned the car round expertly and, with a wave of his hand, disappeared back up the hill. Agnes breathed a sigh of relief and went up to her room to be greeted by an ecstatic Polly. A short walk with the little dog and Agnes was ready for bed. She had enjoyed the visit and the meal and the company. As she sat in front of the dressing-table mirror, removing her make-up, she decided she would ask all three of them to dinner here at the manor. She wondered if Tracey would want to come. Perhaps not. Somehow, the child interested her – the risks she took, stupid risks perhaps, but at fourteen she was managing to live two lives, and live them very successfully, too. If she could do that at her tender age, what would she become as an adult? Maybe something spectacular?

Agnes tried to tell herself the child was taking risks that might lead her into all sorts of trouble, but she couldn't help admiring her, just a little. She hoped she would meet her again.

Just as Agnes was falling asleep, Polly made a flying leap and landed on the bed – no doubt, Agnes thought, punishing her for staying out so long and leaving her alone. Usually Polly left it until two or three in the morning before jumping up on the bed. Agnes moved her feet to give the little dog more room. Before she started to fall asleep again, she found herself wondering whether tomorrow Tracey would again escape out of her window, don her forbidden clothes and run down the hill to meet the boyfriend. Probably she would, but Agnes felt she was not quite interested enough to try and find out. She did think, however, how shocked and horrified her deceived parents would be if they found out, or if she took it on herself to tell them – really in order to protect the child. The thought kept her awake a little longer, then she spoke her mind to Polly, now lying on her back with four feet in the air, wide awake, eyes fixed on her mistress.

'No, Polly, I don't want to get involved. Tracey would never forgive me and probably her parents would not either.' On that resolve she fell asleep.

The next morning Agnes had an appointment to have coffee with an old acquaintance rather than a friend from her days when she was living on the Island. This woman lived in the vicinity of the cottage Agnes had rather fancied. Enid Rawlings always seemed to know about everybody and everything. They had never been close, the mutual interest that had drawn them together being the latest novels, biographies and travel books. Enid was a great reader and a very reliable critic, and although she was in her late seventies, her memory was excellent. She always remembered the author's name, the publisher and some of the reviews.

Agnes was aware that Enid had few close friends. She was very arrogant in her views. Her ideas and opinions were set in concrete and nothing would stop her voicing these opinions no matter who she might hurt or offend.

She also had no feeling for animals. This last had made Agnes come very close to disliking her so the friendship had not flourished and had only consisted of an occasional lunch or cup of tea.

However, Enid would be certain to know the previous occupants of the cottage, why it was not selling quickly, and whether anyone was at the moment considering buying it.

Enid Rawlings' house was 'stockbroker Tudor'. The gardens back and front were beautifully laid out without a trace of imagination, very like the gardens on the front at Ryde. Agnes drove up the immaculate gravel drive, between the neat flowers standing like soldiers.

Enid opened the door to Agnes's ring. She looked exactly the same as she had several years ago – hair its usual colour, usual style, her face slightly plump, well made-up. She air-kissed Agnes on one cheek. She looked past Agnes at the car parked outside.

'Still a Porsche – and a new one, Agnes,' she said.

There was meaning in her voice. What she was saying, but not saying, Agnes well knew – 'Still doing all right money-wise, then, inherited enough for a new Porsche.' It was not a new car but Agnes did not correct her.

'Do come in, it was nice of you to ring me.'

Agnes looked back at her car. She had left both rear windows open about an inch and a half and the car was in the shade. Polly would be quite happy in what Agnes called her 'kennel on wheels', as long as she was not away too long – then she might start barking. Enid, she knew, would not be happy with a dog in her house, walking on her carpets, sniffing around. She ushered Agnes into the sitting room, sunny, pretty and unbelievably tidy. She bustled her guest into a seat.

'I'll just get the coffee, Agnes.'

She left the room, Agnes noting as she did so that in spite of her advanced years she wore her usual high-heeled, pretty shoes. Agnes admired the older woman for still wearing such shoes – she herself always wore flatties, or nearly flatties. She comforted herself by thinking perhaps Enid only wore them while she was in the house or to show off to a visitor.

Enid brought in a tray and set it down on the coffee table. Agnes was standing by the french windows looking at the manicured lawn.

'So you are staying at the Brighstone Manor Hotel? What do you make of it, Agnes? There have been stories . . .'

'Stories? What do you mean, "stories", Enid? Do you mean scandal stories or just anecdotes?'

Enid looked sideways at Agnes, her eyes narrowed. 'Oh, sort of scandal stories – you know, naughty weekends, Mr and Mrs Smith, Mr and Mrs Brown.'

Agnes shook her head. For some reason she felt slightly annoyed, put out: all the pairs she had met at the manor seemed to her very much husband and wife, calculating wedding anniversaries. She said as much to Enid, rather tartly. Then she remembered this was typical of Enid, she loved to start hares. She turned the conversation to the cottage.

'Oh, that place. Did you say a friend of yours was interested in it? Well, she shouldn't be. They've had a lot of trouble with the damp course. Of course, that's only hearsay, I admit. But I expect there is some truth in it.'

Agnes wondered if Enid had an eye on the cottage for a friend herself, or thought of buying it as an investment. She gave up any more enquiries about the property and the conversation went on to their usual topic – books. Agnes was glad when the visit was ended but she couldn't resist asking, as she was bidding Enid goodbye, about her remarks on Brighstone Manor Hotel. Enid tossed her head.

'Agnes, you were always naïve about such things, as I remember. There was a man there, a porter I believe, who blackmailed someone and was beaten up. Of course, it was all hushed up. Things like that always are, aren't they? Drugs were mentioned.'

Agnes drove away, resolving she wouldn't look up Enid

40

again. She had put her right off the cottage and, anyway, the thought of living that near to Enid was worse than the problem of the damp course. Polly welcomed her with enthusiasm. Agnes noticed she was 'tummy rumbling' as she called it. The little dog was very rarely ill but maybe the rather rich meals had upset her. Agnes decided to put her back on to her ordinary food and tell the hotel for the moment no more meat and vegetables and rich gravy. Agnes gave her a short walk – and gave herself a very light lunch in Newport. As she sat in the café she thought about what Enid had said – did she mean that the porter had recognized one or two of the guests who were having an illicit weekend together and tried to get money from them and been set on for his pains? Agnes said to herself, 'Well, serve him right,' but couldn't be quite sure of which person she was thinking about, the pair having the weekend or the blackmailing porter. Perhaps it was just a story invented by Enid to make Agnes uncomfortable. Enid could be capable of that.

The rest of the day passed quietly. Agnes gave herself the luxury of a rest on the bed with a new book which she had bought in Newport, by a favourite author of hers. She was soon absorbed in it and Polly spread out on the bed at her feet, seemingly recovered from her 'rumbles' or almost recovered. Now and again there was a small sound from the dog's tummy but she ate her own pellet meal and when the dog's meal was delivered to the room, Agnes simply accepted it with thanks as usual. She did not want to offend the young porter who always delivered the meal and who always made a great fuss of Polly. She tipped the food into a plastic bag to be got rid of later.

Dinner in the restaurant was not quite as good as usual. Perhaps it was the chef's night off, as one of the guests remarked to Agnes. It was the first meal she had had to criticize and she made up with the dessert, which was waffles with maple syrup and ice cream. One of her favourites. After coffee in the lounge and a short chat with a couple of newly arrived guests, she decided she would walk Polly, just a short walk, then bed and her new book.

Agnes read for quite a long time, at the same time keeping an eye on Polly who was not behaving quite as normal. Although she had spread the protective little blanket on the bed, the dog stayed in her own bed and occasionally got up to stretch out on the carpet. Agnes at last could read no more, she was too sleepy. Polly had settled down and was giving her usual little snore which reassured Agnes. She put her book aside, settled her pillows and put out the light. She looked at her bedside clock before she switched off the light – it was twenty to twelve. Even after the light was switched off the green figures on the clock still glowed in the dark. By the time the luminous numbers had faded away, Agnes was asleep.

She was rudely awakened after what she felt had been a very short time. Polly was scratching frantically at the bedroom door. Agnes glanced at her clock, twenty to one. She grabbed her jogging suit and had it on in seconds. She slipped her feet into a pair of sneakers and had Polly's lead on almost at the same time. That tummy rumble had caught up with Polly, who was a very clean little creature and would not make a mess if she could get out. The door scratching was a desperate measure.

Agnes did not even stop to lock her door behind her. She ran down the stairs and crossed the hall – the night porter, his feet propped up on the reception desk, was leaning back in his chair snoring. He did not stir as Agnes crossed the hall. The front door was locked but the key was in the lock. Agnes let herself out and closed the door quietly behind her, then down the steps and along the drive. She wondered if the big gates were locked. Luckily they were not. A quick run to the base of the familiar hill and up, up, up – Polly rushing along on the extended leash until they reached the little dog's usual lavatory area where she at last stopped and crouched down. There was a small explosion. Agnes could only stand and wait patiently for the result. She was thankful the explosion had not taken place in the bedroom. Dear Polly, she had done her best. Perhaps now all would be well. Agnes hoped so.

The night was warm and the moon was bright. Occasional cloud drifted across it, briefly obliterating the scene round her. Polly was scratching up leaves, probably feeling very relieved. Agnes decided to stay a little longer in case there might be another explosion. As she stood there, she remembered she had not locked her bedroom door back at the hotel, and she had left the front door unlocked as well. The sleeping night porter was not much of a guard – he had not stirred as she had turned the key and left the manor. Perhaps he would wake up later; after all, there was nothing much for him to react to at nearly one in the morning.

Agnes was just about to reel in some of Polly's nylon lead and make for home, when she heard someone or something coming up the path from the main road. Her immediate thought was, Tracey. She shrank back into the shadows. The last thing she wanted was to get involved in the girl's night life. She pulled Polly up to her feet and made the little dog sit quietly while the girl went by. Tracey was walking with some difficulty on the stony, uneven path from the main road. Her shoes, as Agnes remembered, would not be very helpful to such a scramble, such a steep climb. She soon passed Agnes and began to walk up to where her case was hidden. Agnes kept very still, listening.

Tracey's steps became fainter, then stopped. She must have reached the hidden clothes. Agnes moved slightly forward so that she could just see the girl on the other side of the track up to her house. Tracey pulled off her tiny skirt, than her tights – her legs gleamed white in the moonlight. Then she pulled on the tracksuit bottoms and off came the lacy top – black this time. Agnes drew back; she heard the girl breathing rather hard – with anxiety perhaps, as well as exertion. The case was snapped shut and pushed back into its hiding place. Tracey came out and turned into the lane. She was not far from her home – a little climb up the side of the garage, through the window, and she was safe. Once more, Agnes thought, she had managed to deceive her parents. Agnes was about to move out of her concealing trees and shrubs when something stopped her and set her heart racing. It was the sound of someone running, and running fast enough to catch up with Tracey. The boyfriend? Agnes drew back as a dark figure passed her in the lane. Short in stature, dressed in black from head to foot, he wore a thin, zip-up jacket with a hood, the hood drawn up well over the head. He ran on. Agnes put her hand down to Polly and gently held her muzzle to stop her barking. Luckily she did not attempt to.

Had the man run up from the lower road where she had come from, or had he followed Tracey, running up the hill from the main road? Agnes couldn't work it out. Suddenly the footsteps in the lane stopped; there was a short, sharp scream. Agnes tethered Polly to a tree branch and followed the man.

Chapter Five

In the seconds it took Agnes to reach the two struggling figures, she realized why Tracey had only let out one scream. The man holding her, his back to Agnes, had his left arm around the girl's throat and mouth. She couldn't scream again. Neither had heard Agnes approach. As she reached them and was about to tackle the man, he screamed – not a high-pitched scream like the girl's, but a low-pitched, growling sound. He kept his hold round her neck, forcing her backward almost on to the ground, his right hand pulling at her trousers, half turning his victim round.

'Oh, it bites, does it? You've made me bleed, you little bitch. You'll suffer for that!'

As he spoke, something clattered to the ground. The cloud that had been obscuring the moon moved on, letting the light pour down on the fallen object. It lay behind the man's straddled legs. The moonlight made the object look bright and menacing. It was a knife, a knife with a six-inch, shining blade – a kitchen knife with a wooden handle. Agnes picked it up, on top of them now.

What Agnes did next was almost a reflex action. The weapon gave her a feeling of power over the animal she saw in front of her, trying to violate a girl of fourteen. She struck, plunged the knife into the man's back. It pierced quite easily through the thin, silky nylon of his jacket. The pain, or the impact, made him straighten up and try to turn to see who was at his back. It was too late. Agnes withdrew the knife. She had struck him near the vertebrae and had felt the knife hit and slide off bone – the backbone, ribs, she was not sure. The knife was now slightly bloody, but only slightly. She struck again. This time the knife sank in through flesh, his left arm still raised. The moon was covered again and as the man's head turned, Agnes only saw the glitter of his dark eyes, the sweaty forehead.

Tracey scrambled up, sobbing, terrified. She pulled up her trousers, staggered a little and the moon obliged again. The man on the ground did not move. Agnes had withdrawn the weapon and held it in her hand – still bloody.

The girl regained a little composure. Still crying, she raised her head and realized who was standing there. She looked completely astounded.

'Mrs Turner, whatever are you doing here?'

The question was muffled and mixed in with her sobs, which were dying away a little, but she looked down at the body on the ground so near her. She screamed again, but not with such volume.

'Go home, go home quickly, Tracey. Go home.'

Agnes followed the girl as she stumbled up the hill towards her home. She followed her just far enough to see her enter the garden gate. The house was in complete darkness. Nothing had disturbed Tracey's parents. She waited a few seconds, which seemed like hours, and at last saw the girl scramble through her bedroom window. Then she turned, still holding the knife, and went back to where the man lay. Just before she reached him she heard a scraping noise, a sliding noise, and her heart nearly stopped. He must be alive, still moving. There was no sign of him but the sliding, slithering noise continued for a few more seconds. Agnes looked over the side of the hill. The man, alive or dead, had rolled or slipped over the ridge, travelling down the slope about ten yards. The slithering sound had stopped because his jacket had caught on a tree stump. The moon lit the scene and a car, lights blazing, passed below on the main road. The man had twisted round and now lay on his back, the zip in his jeans undone, the hood fallen back to reveal his face turned up to the moon. Agnes recognized him. It was the man who had parked her car when she had first arrived at Brighstone Manor, the man who had twice spoken to her with almost rude familiarity.

Agnes realized she still had the knife in her hand, the blade red with blood. She threw it down the hill towards the body. 'Body' was the word: he looked very dead now. Let whoever finds him, find the knife as well – he deserved to die. She walked down the hill, untied Polly's lead and the dog bounded about with joy at her return. She felt shaky but resolute. All she had to do now was to get back in the hotel, preferably unseen. The big gates opened without trouble, the front door was as she had left it – unlocked and ajar. The reception area was empty. The sleeping night porter was nowhere to be seen. She relocked the front door, crossed the hall and ran up the stairs, Polly pattering up beside her. Her bedroom door too was ajar. She went in, closed the door softly behind her and turned the key in the lock. Agnes felt unbearably tired. Polly was obviously recovered: no tummy rumblings now, and she was asking for something to eat. Agnes took off the lead and collar, and gave her a few biscuits. Then she sank down on the bed and as she sat down she felt her hands trembling. She had just killed a man. What would Tracey make of it? Surely she would tell her parents; surely she would have to, though by the look of it they had heard nothing. If she did tell them, all her secrets would come out, too – the boyfriend, the clubs or wherever they went, the drugs maybe? Agnes felt the girl was strong enough to keep this whole incident to herself. She was only fourteen but seemed to have a self-control and determination that belied her years. Very little love for her parents.

. As she sat there on the side of the bed, other fears crept in. Supposing he was not dead, would he recover lying there on the hill – call out, make someone hear him, tell them what happened? She was almost sure that he had not seen her face, his back had been towards her the whole time – or had he just caught a glimpse of her before he fell, recognized her? No, she was sure, sure, sure he was dead.

Wearily she took off her jogging suit. Luckily it didn't seem to have any blood on it. She felt cold, chilled. She had a quick shower, put on pyjamas and got into bed. She looked at Polly; Polly looked at her, and then took her usual leap on to the bed, tail wagging, feet in the air. Agnes stroked the dog's head, trying to calm herself.

'All this happened because of you, Polly.'

Polly's brown eyes looked at her as if she understood.

'When, or if, he doesn't turn up for work tomorrow, what will they say? He'll hardly be able to send a sick note, will he?'

Polly wagged her tail but did not reply. Agnes turned out the light. The moon was hidden by cloud now, and rain began to patter on her window.

In the morning when Agnes woke she was surprised how well she had slept, even though the night, her night, had been short. As she dressed after Polly's little walk, she felt apprehensive. What would she find when she went downstairs to the dining room? Would there be uproar, the police, the guests exchanging views and expressions of horror and disbelief about the body found on the hill so near to the hotel? Agnes almost decided to skip breakfast, go back to her room and miss all the drama, if, of course, there was any drama.

She need not have worried. When she reached the dining room she was greeted with the usual cheery 'Good morning, Mrs Turner' from the waitress who served her table. She sat down and was conscious for the first time how the tension had got to her this morning in spite of sleeping. She ordered juice and coffee and toast. While she waited she found herself thankful for one or two things. First, she had not told anyone that Polly had had an upset tummy and needed urgently to be taken out, and secondly, no one had seen her leave or return to the hotel last night. The absence of the night porter, his being asleep, was all

48

good luck for her. She thought as she waited that she must plot a little. She would not cancel the meals they brought up to her room for Polly. She would not let her eat them, just get rid of them and return the empty plate with her usual thanks. She would feed Polly her food pellets. Anyway, the little dog was completely recovered. Agnes said a little prayer that there would not have to be any more night walks. It had poured with rain last night after she and Polly had got safely back into her room. A glance out of the dining-room window showed the still dripping trees and the small, shining pools on the front lawns. The man's body, if it was still there, would be soaked now and the knife washed clean of blood.

The orange juice, coffee, toast and butter and marmalade arrived. The waitress smiled at her again, all seemed normal. But Agnes could not help her thoughts drifting forward. Not long, surely, before the body was found, already he must be missing from his daily stint of work?

Then the man at the next table said to his companion, a fat, comfortable-looking lady, 'That man – you know, he was going to clean the car today, this morning before we go to your mother's. Well, he's not turned up for work. The receptionist told me.'

'Oh, never mind, dear, the rain will have given it a good wash – probably saved our money.'

Agnes smiled. The fat, comfortable lady had just made a fat, comfortable reply. She was always pleased when someone acted in accordance with their appearance.

She wondered if the house on the hill was as quiet and normal as the hotel. Had Tracey told her parents she had almost been raped, but, thanks to Mrs Turner, had been saved . . .? Agnes decided that in a while she would telephone and ask them to dinner later in the week. She would be able to tell at once if they knew anything about last night's happenings. She looked at her watch: nine thirty – a little too early to ring yet. She got up, collected her *Telegraph* from the hall and took it up to her room. She

49

lay down on the bed and tried to read, but her concentration was disturbed.

Was he dead? Had he been dead when he had slithered down the hill? When and how would he be found? Days, weeks, months – would he be left there to rot? One thing she felt almost certain about: Tracey would not tell her parents. She had crept into that dark house, sobbing, shaking as Agnes had seen her, but giving nothing away. To tell them that she had been out at that time of night or morning would entail sacrificing so much: the boyfriend, the parties, the clubbing, even the source of the drugs that maybe she relied on? No, she would not tell. The portrait of herself the girl had manufactured had taken a great deal of effort, too much effort to give away easily: the perfect daughter – obedient, co-operative, good at school, swotting for her exams. Agnes thought of her own subservient youth and gave the girl ten out of ten for guts. She herself could never have kept up such a charade. Not, at any rate, when she was still only fourteen years old.

It was twenty past ten when Agnes decided to telephone the Rymans. Thelma Ryman, as she had expected, answered the telephone. There was no sign of agitation, no *'What do you think, Agnes? They have found the body of a man on the hill down the road, not very far from our house. Isn't it horrible?'* Nothing like that.

'Oh, Agnes, how nice to hear your voice. What a wet day, and what a downpour! It's clearing up now and there is even a bit of blue sky and sunshine.'

Agnes explained her reason for the call, suggesting they might like to come to dinner at the manor on Thursday or Friday evening. Thelma sounded genuinely pleased by the invitation.

'Oh yes, we would love to come. All of us. My husband's gone to the golf club – maybe it will be too wet to play but he likes to be there among his friends and players. Tracey is at school, but I am sure I can accept for them both.'

'Seven o'clock? Then we can have a drink at the bar.

Polly's allowed in the bar and she has already made a few doggy friends there, so she doesn't feel too left out. In fact, she enjoys it.'

'Oh, lovely – then we'll be able to see the dear girl.'

Agnes put the phone down, not sure if she was more pleased or worried that nobody had yet discovered the body.

She decided not to take Polly up the hill with its rather intimidating connotations, but to motor up to Brading Down and perhaps lunch there as well. The weather had improved and the sun was shining and warming the late morning. The dripping trees and shrubs were drying and the little pools on the lawns were gradually disappearing. Agnes walked to the car, savouring the freshness of the wet grass. She did wonder, though, when she came back after lunch, would the scene be as peaceful and serene, or would they have found him? She got into the Porsche with Polly and drove away, feeling relieved for the moment to be able to turn her back on the place. When they found the body it would be soon enough to remember last night again. Agnes had been slightly apprehensive that Thelma Ryman might have suggested that she walk up the hill and have a coffee with her – luckily she had not done so. She did not fancy the idea of climbing up that hill again for some time. The Porsche gave her a feeling of reassurance and freedom.

Thelma had decided on Thursday, if that would suit Agnes? It would. Although Agnes was not particularly looking forward to the date, she was always punctilious about returning invitations. Thelma Ryman seemed to Agnes a much nicer person than either her husband or her daughter. Her husband was pompous and rather dictatorial, and what she had witnessed of the young one's behaviour had prejudiced her. She seemed to be deceiving everyone.

Sitting in the car on Brading Down, she let her thoughts wander back to the days when she had lived on the Island, all the things, happy and sad, that had happened. She

51

decided not to bother with lunch but bought an ice cream cornet with a chocolate flake stuck in the middle. She felt reluctant to return to the manor and drove round the country roads for about an hour before she set off for the hotel, stopping at a little café on the way for a cup of tea. It was ten past five when she eventually arrived back. All was quiet.

The scene was the same as when she had left – no police, no police cars with flashing lights, no cordoned-off road. He must still be there, soaked with last night's rain, still lying spread-eagled, head towards the road below, sightless eyes turned to the lacy tangle of the tree branches above him, the sun shining on his face, unaware of cold or warmth. Agnes parked her Porsche and walked through the hall. The receptionist greeted her with a warm smile. Agnes had been there longer now than any of the other guests, except for one permanent aged lady who spoke to no one and appeared to live there. Agnes was rather a favourite guest: she was a good tipper and polite to everybody, particularly the staff. Polly was a favourite, too. Agnes accepted her key and went upstairs to her room. Polly's meal was delivered. The little dog smelled the meat and her nose twitched, but she didn't seem at all disappointed or put out by the dish of pellet food that Agnes put down for her. She tucked into it with enthusiasm.

Agnes put the unwanted meal in a plastic bag and tied up the top so that she could dispose of it tomorrow. Then she put the plate outside her door to be collected. As she did so, she felt a bit deceitful, the kitchen really took trouble making up nice meals for the visitors' dogs, but she could not risk another upset tummy and have to take Polly out late at night or early in the morning. Once had been enough, and particularly now she wanted to keep away from the hill altogether.

Agnes changed her dress, repaired her make-up and brushed her hair vigorously, a touch of her Joy perfume and she was ready for her visit to the bar. She enjoyed this nightly gathering, enjoyed all the dogs being there – a

Dobermann had made himself famous the other evening by drinking half a pint of beer with obvious enjoyment. It was a matey and convivial atmosphere. So far there had not been a dog-fight. She was determined to introduce the Rymans to the bar atmosphere when they arrived on Thursday. It was a good way of breaking the ice. She gave Polly a brush, put on her lead and made her way down the stairs and through towards the bar. As she reached the bottom of the stairs, a police siren blared out. Agnes jumped and her heart began to race. Then she realized the sound of the police car was coming from the sitting room off the hall – the television room. Agnes glanced through the open door and could see on the screen a police car's lights flashing, the car tearing along the road. She calmed down, but it brought home to her how tense she was, waiting for the discovery.

She walked into the bar and the dogs and the humans greeted each other. Agnes ordered a brandy and ginger ale. Normally before dinner she drank white wine, but this evening she felt in need of something stronger. She must watch her emotions and reactions. If there were suddenly sounds of police cars going by the hotel, or police entering the hotel, she must show exactly the right amount of surprise and curiosity. She must certainly not let anyone suspect she knew what was happening, what had been discovered on the hill, before it was public knowledge. That might well be a fatal giveaway – that is, of course, if anyone noticed her lack of surprise.

Maureen and Martin James were still staying at Brighstone Manor. They liked it so much they had extended their stay for another two weeks. Martin was retired and told Agnes he thought he needed this restful holiday to 'wind down', as he put it. Maureen always looked slightly doubtful when he said this. Agnes suspected that perhaps she would like a more exciting holiday and didn't have her husband's need to 'wind down'. Perhaps she would rather have gone abroad.

Eventually everybody migrated to the dining room and

their separate tables, and not a siren or a policeman invaded the serving of the first course. Agnes, however, could not quite reduce her tension. It must happen, he must be found soon. Admittedly the body was not directly on the path down to the road, but it was only a short distance away from that path. Few people used it, but it would be found. Agnes could almost visualize it. *'A man walking his dog saw the body and reported it to the police.'* No one in the hotel had even mentioned the porter's absence except to say that he was not very reliable. Agnes tried to dismiss it from her mind, but if she did not discipline herself she could feel again the plunge of the knife partially deflected by bone, perhaps the rib, then the second plunge through soft tissue – more effective. She felt absolutely no remorse. Any man who could rape a young girl deserved what he got. He deserved to be 'rubbed out', taken out of society – not given a short sentence in a comfortable prison, then let out to do exactly the same if he felt so inclined. No, she was right. That side of the incident did not make her feel in the least remorseful.

Chapter Six

Agnes knew that the body had been found before she opened her eyes the following morning. The lights flashing on the police cars flashed, too, on her closed eyelids and wakened her. She knew immediately and turned away from the window, reluctant to open her eyes, but she couldn't shut them to what was going on outside for ever. She had to face this morning, answer any questions the police might ask. She looked at her bedside clock. Gleaming weakly, it read twenty past seven. Surely, she thought, it should be lighter? Agnes swung her legs out of bed, put on her jogging suit and crossed over to the window. No wonder it was dark – the sky was black and stormy, the rain pouring down. Great, big storm drops.

Polly, disturbed by the noise and the talking of the police, their feet crunching on the gravel of the drive, was scratching at the door, more out of curiosity than a need to relieve herself. Agnes put on stout shoes and reached for the mackintosh in her wardrobe – the first time she had had to use it since the start of her little holiday. Polly would have to make do with Pooh Corner this morning, and not go anywhere near the hill. She snapped on Polly's lead, closed her door behind her, locked it, crossed the upstairs hall and made her way down the stairs. Her heart was beating a little faster than normal. There were no policemen in the downstairs hall, but a tall, thin man in a rather smart suit was talking to the receptionist. Agnes could hear a hoover being used in the television room. The whole hotel seemed to be up and moving about. Breakfast did not start until eight thirty – the lights were on because of the stormy weather. As Agnes passed the man at the reception desk, she noticed he had the registration book in front of him and was slowly reading the pages, a pair of half glasses perched on his nose. As Agnes passed he turned and looked at her and murmured a polite 'Good morning', then walked away towards the television room. As he entered the hoovering stopped abruptly. A harassed-looking woman came out of the room pushing the machine and holding the lead loosely in her hand, rather as if she had left in a hurry because she had been told to.

Agnes pulled the hood of her mackintosh well over her head and made her way out into the garden. The swimming pool's surface was peppered and splashing with big raindrops. Polly looked slightly disgusted and glanced up at Agnes as if to say, 'You don't expect me to do anything in this, do you? Let's go back and wait until the rain stops.' In spite of this, Polly found a fairly dry place under a half fallen-down chicken coop. She took some time in this procedure, scratching round in the dry earth, smelling the rotting wood with a good deal of enjoyment. Agnes, meanwhile, stood in the pouring rain, waiting with her usual patience whenever an animal was concerned. She had to admit to herself she hadn't the same feelings for humans and never did have.

Through the trees beyond the area she could see the yellow-coated policemen walking about at the base of the hill and on the main road. She wondered if they would question everyone in the Manor Hotel. Well, she was well rehearsed in what she intended to say.

A man with two black Labradors bid her a hasty good morning, well covered in mac and hood, and a high-laced pair of boots. He looked rather like something from outer space. He kept his head well down against the rain and waited with great patience while his dogs, obviously liking the conditions, were chasing about, getting muddier and muddier. Agnes commiserated with his plight and he raised his head from beneath his hood, rather like a tortoise, shrugging his shoulders and saying by way of explanation, 'Well, you see, Mrs Turner, they're gundogs.' Agnes could just see the connection, but gathered up Polly under one arm and made her way back through the soaking garden to the hotel, glad to be going in.

Back in her room, Agnes dried Polly, gave her a token breakfast biscuit, and filled up her water dish. She felt slightly apprehensive about going downstairs again. She had a quick shower and put on a rather becoming light, tweedy trouser suit, suitable she felt for today's weather. She made her face up carefully, surveyed herself for some minutes in the dressing-table mirror, then went out, locked her door and made her way downstairs. If she was going to be questioned by the police she wanted to look her best. Good clothes and well-applied make-up, she always felt, gave her confidence and poise. As she descended the stairs, she tried to imagine what possible things the police could touch on. She had not heard or seen anything unusual, but is that the kind of question they would ask? It was hard to imagine much else.

To her surprise everything appeared as normal. She went through to the dining room where a few tables were occupied and sat down at her usual table.

'What's happening, Maria? What are all these police doing here? The police cars woke me.' She gazed, her expression all innocence, at the girl. 'Has there been a burglary or something?'

'Oh, Mrs Turner, much worse than that. They found our porter, Hugh his name is – I mean was. Hugh Watkins – he used to park the cars for guests, you know?'

Agnes nodded, her expression turning to subdued horror. She waited for the next piece of news, eyebrows raised.

'They found him dead at the bottom of the hill – well, nearly at the bottom, just above the main road. The bus driver found him – the early bus. It was so dark he had his headlights on and when he came round the curve, the

57

lights showed poor Hughie lying there in the rain, dead. It must have been awful.'

Agnes had time to think while the girl was talking. Just above the main road? The body must have slipped much further down after she had left it, caught by the jacket on a tree stump or something. Then she remembered the rain, the pouring rain that had started after she had got safely back to her bedroom that night, or rather early the next morning. Probably the hill was a sea of mud by now, slippery, sodden, water drifting down the path.

The waitress suddenly burst into tears and took out from her pocket a crumpled tissue to dry her eyes, already red and swollen.

'It's awful. I didn't like him, Mrs Turner, he tried it on, you know, all the time no matter how much you put him off. But I wouldn't like anyone to die like that, would you?'

Agnes made a rather mild reply to this: 'No, of course I wouldn't but we don't know how he died yet, do we, Maria?'

The girl shook her head and wiped more tears away. 'The policeman asked me if I had heard anything; how well I knew Hugh and stuff like that. I didn't say he tried it on sometimes – well, I mean, he won't try it on any more, will he?'

She suddenly seemed to remember that Agnes was sitting there waiting for her breakfast and gave a last wipe to her eyes.

'Oh, I'm sorry, Mrs Turner, I'll get your breakfast. Things seem to be all over the place this morning.'

She walked away from the table and was almost at the door to the kitchen when she turned and came back to Agnes, still dabbing her eyes with the wet tissue.

'I forgot to ask you, orange juice, coffee and toast, or would you like a cooked breakfast?'

Agnes's patience was beginning to ebb a little. 'No, Maria, just what I usually have, please.'

The girl nodded, hesitated as if she was going to say

something else, decided against it and this time made it through into the kitchens. The drama of it all had rather taken over, Agnes thought, amused.

While Agnes was eating, one or two people came in, full of curiosity about what was going on, why the police? Two elderly ladies, who Agnes had thought would have left by now, seemed not only quite firmly entrenched, but also a little annoyed that their morning had been disturbed. Maria, who served their table too, was just about to fill them in with the details she had gleaned, when she was interrupted by a young man emerging from the television room. He was young and looked slightly embarrassed at having to address the assembled breakfast eaters. He fiddled with his tie and peered at the clipboard in his hand, hesitating and clearing his throat.

'The Detective Inspector has asked me to have a word with you as you leave. Just routine.'

He lowered the clipboard and nodded towards the television room. There were one or two murmurs.

'The hotel has kindly lent us the room . . .'

He tailed off and disappeared into the appointed room, to be followed by a policeman in the usual yellow gear and soaking wet cap and trousers. Agnes let one or two people go into the room and come out again unscathed. The owner of the two Labradors seemed out of temper. Perhaps, Agnes thought, it was the soaking he had received earlier on when he was walking his dogs in Pooh Corner.

'Waste of time, of course. I didn't hear anything,' he said.

He stamped rather angrily from the dining room, muttering to himself.

A young, pretty, fair-haired policewoman was talking earnestly to an elderly couple seated at a table at the other end of the dining room. She motioned with her hand towards the television room. The couple nodded in agreement, the woman gathered up her handbag and picked up the cardigan flung over the back of her chair. She looked rather anxiously at her husband; he touched her arm and probably said something reassuring to her.

The policewoman approached Agnes's table. Her youth and freshness made the uniform she wore look perfect: the crisp white blouse, dark skirt, black stockings, well-polished shoes, the tie at the neck. Agnes stood up as she got nearer.

'I wonder, Mrs Turner, if you could spare a moment to have a word with DI Marriot – just routine. He wants to have a word with everyone in the hotel, staff and guests, just in case anyone saw or heard anything.'

Agnes agreed at once and resumed her seat to wait for the elderly couple to come out. She smiled at the police-woman, who walked away to speak to another young couple who had just entered the room and were being shown to their table by Debbie, one of the other waitresses. The elderly couple emerged, talking to each other, looking very serious. Coming away for a relaxing break, Agnes thought, and then being questioned about a murder not all that far away, was quite an experience for them. One expected Miss Marple to appear at any moment!

Agnes walked rather slowly across the dining room. The policewoman came up to her, smiling.

'Would you like to see DI Marriot, Mrs Turner?'

Agnes nodded and smiled back at her. She felt more at ease now. 'I'm afraid I won't be very helpful but I will certainly answer any questions he asks.'

The Detective Inspector stood up as she came into the room and indicated the chair on the opposite side of the table at which he was sitting. Agnes was quite right about the questions – had she seen anything on the night, had she heard anything? Did she know the man who had been killed? Agnes could only say no to all the questions. She told DI Marriot that the man had parked her car for her when she had first arrived, had taken her luggage up to her room, but as far as she could remember that was the only time she had any contact with him. She omitted her two other meetings with him. What possible connection could there be, she asked herself, so judged it better to say nothing at all. After a very few minutes the policeman stood up and extended a hand to Agnes. She was about to leave when she suddenly remembered her dinner date with the Rymans. She felt she should mention it.

'Oh, Inspector, I have asked three people to a meal tomorrow evening. Will the path be open? I noticed you have some of your ribbons stretched across the access to their house?'

'Of course. The obstruction will be gone by tomorrow morning. Please let them and the hotel know it will be quite in order for them to come.'

Agnes left the room, deciding she would telephone the Rymans straight away, let them know it was OK. Perhaps they would not care to come. The police, while questioning Agnes about her walks up the hill and her becoming friendly with the Rymans, seemed rather uninterested. The walk up the hill was used by several people with their dogs. Agnes had asked who had found the body and the policeman had been quite open about the discovery. Apparently the bus driver, driving to Newport early to get something done to his engine, had his lights on as the morning was so dark and rain pouring down. As he drove around a slight curve in the road his headlights had picked out the body, the face really, within a foot or so of the path beside the road. According to Maria, the driver was quite upset. He rang the police on his mobile and waited for them to arrive. Agnes listened with interest. The body must have slid nearly all the way down to the road below. Agnes wondered had he moved, had he been alive and so managed to move? She didn't think so. It was the wet leaves and the mud that had made a perfect slide. The nylon coat must have torn away from where it had suspended the body. Anyway, he was dead.

Thelma Ryman answered Agnes's telephone call. She sounded delighted that the dinner date was still on.

'Richard is terribly upset about this awful business. He has calmed down a bit now but at first he wanted to sell the house, move away from here. He wants to stay on the Island because of his beloved golf club. Tracey told him not to be silly – what a sensible girl my daughter is, Agnes!'

Agnes made casual remarks about how the young found it easier to deal with these crises than the more mature, etc. etc.

'Well, we will talk about it tomorrow, Agnes. I am so looking forward to seeing you – we all are. It will be so nice to get away from the house.'

Agnes drew her own conclusions, having heard Thelma: Tracey had said nothing, kept her own counsel. If she admitted she had been attacked she would be grounded, her parents would hardly let her out of their sight. So many things Agnes wondered about Tracey, a whole list of queries she hoped to solve when she met the girl at dinner. How they would be able to manage a conversation with her parents there, Agnes didn't know, but she was determined to ask her. Had she managed to secrete the case of clothes back into her home without the police knowing? Had she managed to get in touch with her boyfriend? If she told all, including Agnes's involvement, she would almost certainly lose everything she seemed to value enough to take risks for.

At the moment there were two or three yellow-clad policemen scratching about the hill, slipping and sliding on the mud of the meagre pathway down the slope to the main road. All the hotel staff had been interviewed several times. Some of the guests had been allowed to leave and a few new ones had arrived. The rain stopped at last, and Agnes took herself off to an auction sale in Ryde, giving Polly a rather wet walk on the way. The auction room was full and smelled of wet mackintoshes. Agnes enjoyed it.

That evening, after dinner, she watched television, Polly on her knee. The news interested her, particularly the Southern News: a stabbing in Bournemouth, another in Southampton, a man taken to hospital with multiple injuries after being set on outside a club in Newport. It's all go, she thought with a wry smile. Our killing looks like being one of quite a few.

'Did you say something, dear, I'm a little deaf?'

Agnes did not realize she had been thinking aloud. 'No, nothing at all. Just talking to myself.'

The Brighstone murder was not mentioned.

The next day Agnes found boring: she realized she was waiting to meet the Rymans, particularly Tracey. The local paper included a rather sketchy piece about the murder – probably because the police had not thought it politic to reveal too much before they had found out a little more about the stabbing. As far as she could make out, they had not discovered the weapon. Agnes thought of those poor souls, the policemen, sliding about on that hill, mud up to their elbows, searching for that kitchen knife. What did it matter exactly what had killed him? He was a rapist – any weapon was a good weapon. As to fingerprints, rain and maybe blood would have obliterated those, she was pretty certain. She remembered the handle had been made of wood – not good material to retain prints, she had read in many murder trials, especially if soaked through and through with that endless rain.

Agnes gave Polly two very good walks that she felt would make up for the bad weather which had kept her in. She even had tea in the manor to help pass the time until her guests arrived. As she drank her tea in the large lounge, only the resident old lady was in the room with her. Agnes looked at her critically, wondering to herself would she one day be sitting, drinking tea, in similar circumstances – old, deaf, happier to live like this in a hotel with plenty of people to look after you? Nothing to do all day except wait for the next meal and eventually moving into a residential home with almost everything done for you. Agnes felt depression, her old enemy, closing down on her. She tried to shrug it off, poured herself another cup of tea. Maria came into the room to see if she had finished with her tea tray. When she saw Agnes was still drinking, she lingered beside her chair longing to tell her thoughts about the local drama to anyone who would listen.

'You know what I think, Mrs Turner? I believe it was some husband whose wife Hughie had been having it off with, you know.'

Getting no reply from Agnes she went on with her idea: 'I mean, as I said, he was like that, not flirting exactly but really coming on to you, you know?'

Agnes nodded and surrendered her tray to Maria. Hughie was a nasty piece of work, what did he matter? She thought this but did not say it.

Maria's short conversation had done something to disperse Agnes's encroaching depression, brought on by the sight of the old lady. No, she would never get like that, never. There was always something coming up in her life to make it worthwhile. Always someone, or something, to be disposed of.

A short walk for Polly, then she would have a shower, put on her pale green dress that she had not worn here yet – her favourite; then the Rymans and their reactions to the murder and the police questions, and Tracey's – most of all Tracey's – behaviour. How would she react, particularly towards herself? The secret between the two of them would surely be a little electric?

The green dress slid over her head and down her body. It still fitted her perfectly. Make-up – very discreet, but the eyeshadow slightly noticeable, matching the pale, tender green of the dress. Agnes felt good. A gentle puff of Joy and she was ready. She twirled once more in front of the mirror and, satisfied, she patted Polly, locked her door and made her way downstairs, the little dog pattering beside her, tethered on her short lead.

Chapter Seven

Agnes crossed the hall with Polly as the Rymans' car drew up at the front door. She was not at all surprised to see they had come by car: the walk back up the hill to their house was quite a pull and Thelma had made one or two references to her backache. A new porter went down the steps to the car. Richard Ryman handed him the keys to enable him to park the car for them. Shades of the dead Hughie, Agnes thought – how quickly the water regains its normal surface and the ripples die away. So it should be with such a man, better gone than here. There was no sign of Tracey – perhaps she would arrive later.

The evening was bright and sunny, the lawns green and springy, no hint of the drenching rain that had poured down a day or two ago. Thelma greeted Polly with enthusiasm and the ever-welcoming little dog returned the greeting. Richard seemed only able to look around him with astonishment, and make remarks like, 'By George, this place has pulled its socks up! We haven't been here since your mother was living in the house, before we took over – do you remember, Thelma? It's really something now.'

The receptionist caught Agnes's eye as they passed through the hall on their way to the bar. She made a little face at Agnes, probably Richard's remarks about the improvements that had been made rankled a little. Perhaps she had been on the staff in the old days. None too tactful, perhaps, our Richard. Agnes smiled back at the receptionist and shrugged her shoulders. She hoped it would not offend the girl too much; they had become quite friendly during Agnes's stay and she wanted to keep it that way.

The bar was fairly full as usual at that time in the evening. Agnes led her guests to a table. Thelma was more interested in the dogs than the people – the two handsome, dignified golden retrievers claimed her attention at first, but not for long. Polly danced up to one of them, perhaps the older of the two, and the retriever's lip rose dangerously, showing its menacing white teeth. Polly, quick to take the hint, backed away and leapt up on to the plastic seat beside Thelma and cuddled up against her, her eyes focused on Thelma's face as if she was saying, 'Protection, please, did you see how he threatened me?' The two black Labradors, friendly and tail-wagging, moved around the bar, leads dragging, mouths smiling special Labrador smiles as they accepted the odd crisp when their master wasn't looking their way.

'Oh, isn't it lovely in here, Richard. I love it, all these dogs – so warm and friendly. And what a nice bar!'

A young 'teenage' Dobermann came in with a young couple, skirted carefully around the golden retrievers and settled, upside down, legs in the air, under the man's stool at the bar. More cause for Thelma's delight. Her joy in animals endeared her to Agnes.

'And no fighting, Agnes!' she said.

She drank orange juice, an indication that she was driving, Agnes thought. Richard had another whisky and soda, Agnes a second gin and tonic. Just as they were starting their second drink the glamorous blonde Agnes had seen in the bar a few nights ago arrived with her white lion-clipped poodle. She climbed on to a bar stool, showing quite a large amount of thigh. Her blonde hair, when it fell back a little from her face, revealed a slightly lined but well made-up face. She delved in her large, black, expensive-looking handbag and paid for her drink. The poodle, obviously a dog who liked to be noticed, scratched at the stool. The blonde sipped her drink, then lent down, picked up the dog and placed it on the vacant stool beside her. In front of its nose was a small glass dish full of salted peanuts. The dog polished them off in seconds, grinding the nuts up with sharp white teeth.

'Naughty girl, they weren't for you, darling.' The blonde smiled at the barman, blinking her eyelashes. She finished her drink, picked up the dog and walked out of the bar, leaving most of the guests speechless. The barman removed the glass dish, cast his eyes heavenwards and made no comment. Thelma's reaction was, to Agnes, quite typical.

'Oh, Agnes, you don't think the poor little thing was hungry, do you? To eat all those nuts?'

Agnes shook her head and tried to reassure her. At that moment the waiter came in from the dining room: 'Mrs Turner, your table is ready.'

They all got up, Richard swallowing the remainder of his whisky and soda in a hurried gulp. Agnes followed the waiter to the door then turned to her guests, pointing toward the table by the window, indicating they follow him.

'I must just take Polly up to my room, she's not allowed in the dining room, I'm afraid.'

On the way upstairs, Polly scampered beside her. Ready for her supper, Agnes thought as she let herself into her room. What a joy it had been that not a word had been said, while they had their pre-dinner drinks, about the murder or the police search. She had half expected people to chatter about it, or express opinions about it, but no, not a word. Surely Thelma had been a bit boring about the dogs, but Agnes, of course, could forgive her that.

Polly fed and watered, Agnes locked the door behind her and went down to join her guests. As she arrived at the table she noticed that the waiter, as instructed, had poured the red wine Agnes had chosen, but Richard's glass was empty and he had pushed it away a little. Agnes guessed he was probably no wine drinker so she immediately suggested he would perhaps like a whisky instead.

Richard's face brightened at once and the drink was supplied. Thelma seemed happy with the wine.

The whole dinner was undoubtedly a success. The starter, a fish platter, went down well. The absence of Tracey was hardly mentioned. Agnes understood this, the visit to the bar would have been difficult as would Tracey's attitude to food. Although she had included the girl in the invitation, she was slightly relieved when she didn't turn up. At the end of the meal the three went through to the lounge for coffee and liqueurs.

'Very warm and comfortable, Agnes. You have done us really proud.'

Richard, after four whiskies and a liqueur, was feeling no pain and was completely relaxed. Thelma suddenly remembered something, snapped open her handbag and delved inside, pulling out a small white envelope.

'Oh, Agnes, Tracey gave me a note, a card for you, by way of an apology, I think. So like her, isn't it? She's staying with her friend Denise in Newport tonight.'

She handed Agnes an envelope. It was sealed. Then Agnes noticed two strips of scotch tape had been stuck over the opening as well. She popped it into her own handbag, thinking she would open it later. It was polite of the girl to send it – but Agnes was also curious to know whether Tracey would have made any reference to that terrible night.

The Rymans eventually took their leave, full of thanks and enthusiasm. Their car was brought to the door for them. Thelma, much to Agnes's relief, got into the driver's seat and Agnes waved as they disappeared, their red tail lights fading away. Thelma had managed to persuade Agnes to walk up and have a coffee with her the next day. Agnes was agreeable; she would be able to hear more about the police attitude toward the murder of Hughie Watkins; Tracey's reactions; Richard's – all of interest to Agnes. However, tomorrow was tomorrow. She was pleased how the dinner had gone. Meanwhile, there was

Polly to take for her comfort walk and then get ready for bed. Agnes looked at her watch – ten to eleven.

It was twenty past eleven when at last Agnes could cuddle down with Polly in her place on the bed and her new book in her hand. She felt sleepy: a very short read would be quite enough to make her drop off. She was just starting to read when she remembered the card, Tracey's card. Should she get out of bed and retrieve the envelope from her handbag? She half decided no, then roused herself, got up, took the card from her bag and slipped back into bed, pulled off the scotch tape, tore back the flap and opened the small, pretty card. All thought of sleep was banished as she read it.

On the blank side was written in a round, childish hand:

Thanks for the invite, Mrs Turner.
Not my scene, though.
Staying with Denise, my friend.
Revising for exams. Some revising!
Managed to get my case in without anyone seeing it. Clever, no?

The opposite page was divided in the middle by a large, gold-printed *Thank You*. It was the message written above and below this in the same schoolgirlish handwriting – this was the message that made Agnes sit up straight in her bed and desert her relaxed position on her pillows:

Would you get me four pairs of fishnet tights from Pop Shop, Newport. I think they are seven fifty or so a pair.
Send to the address below.

This referred to a small sticker giving, apparently, the place to send the tights, where Tracey was staying – Denise's house.

Agnes read the card carefully once again, then relaxed back on to her pillows. She was angry.

69

'Blackmailing, Polly, naughty girl! She doesn't know quite who she is dealing with, does she?'

Polly wagged her tail in complete sympathy. Agnes picked up her book but did not resume reading. She gazed across the room, her heart beating just a trace more quickly. It was so nice to have an aim again, a challenge. She had been peaceful for too long, far too long. Blackmailers never stopped, were never satisfied with something demanded. Later something more. Endless.

Next morning broke with a new sensation of excitement. At first, she did not remember quite why she felt so different. Then her eyes took in the little envelope on her bedside table and she understood her feeling.

The girl, the nearly fifteen-year-old girl, whom she had saved from rape, had to be dealt with and, knowing herself, she knew that the dealing would banish her depression, her feeling of boredom, her need – always there too – to justify her life. Agnes knew perfectly well she would do whatever she deemed appropriate. The feeling when it came always frightened her a little as well as excited her. She was glad she had accepted Thelma Ryman's invitation to coffee this morning. She felt she had questions to ask, motives to explore. Had the Rymans heard anything on that fatal night? Had Tracey said anything, acted any differently? Agnes got out of bed, giving Polly a little hug as she did so – Polly, her accomplice?

'Things to do, Polly, at last, things to do.'

After breakfast Agnes drove to Newport. She managed, after a little trouble, to find the shop Tracey had named. She bought four pairs of the requested black fishnet tights. The assistant who served her was a rather spotty, unattractive young woman who showed absolutely no interest in the purchase, chewed gum the whole time she was serving Agnes and, after giving Agnes her change, retired to a chair behind a concealing rack of clothes where she was engrossed in a magazine. Agnes had time to notice the picture on the front cover – a young man in full male glory with biceps to match. She then went back to the post office, bought a suitable envelope to hold the tights, copied the address on the sticky label, paid the required first class postage, affixed the stamps and dropped the package in the mail box. As Agnes did so, she wondered what would be the next demand, or would there be none at all? Would a fourteen-year-old act in the way a blackmailer normally did, making her demands bigger as they went along? Tracey probably watched television enough to pick up criminal ideas. Agnes wondered if Denise, the friend, was of similar type – was she deceiving her parents? Thelma might be able to tell her more about Denise and her parents. Probably Thelma and Richard felt that their sweet-mannered, perfect daughter could only be a good, even perfect influence on her friends, teaching them by example how to be everything a parent wanted. Agnes had no doubt Tracey could teach this Denise the ways of her world. Would she tell Denise or anyone the horrific truth? No, if Agnes felt certain of anything, it was Tracey's ability to keep her own counsel – just as she did herself.

At half-past ten Agnes started to walk up the hill towards the Rymans' house – Polly was delighted to be back on her own, well-known walk again. A couple of policemen passed her, said 'Good morning' but did not challenge her in any way. As she passed the place where the body had slid down in the mud and leaves, she noticed a square at the bottom of the hill, almost by the roadside, surrounded by the familiar yellow and blue ribbon with 'Police' written on it at intervals. No police down there. Agnes wondered if the knife had been found – there had been no mention of it in the paper.

Thelma Ryman opened the door before Agnes had time to press the bell. Both Polly and Agnes got the same greeting. Perhaps Polly got more stroking and patting, though Thelma did clasp Agnes's hand and lean forward to give her a peck on the cheek. Agnes, not one to like particularly tactile greetings, put up with it and tried to return the kiss and to recover her normal reserve. She had a suspicion that Thelma was a rather lonely woman. Her husband seemed very self-sufficient and her daughter more than capable of living a life within her own boundaries, which did not really include anything else but her own desires.

'I thought, as it's such a lovely morning, we could have coffee in the conservatory, then Polly can run about and explore the garden. It's quite safe and enclosed – she can't get out at all. Is that all right, Agnes?'

The conservatory was pretty and flower-filled, largely, Agnes thought, because of Thelma's efforts. She sat down by the wicker table. The chair, which was made of the same material, was comfortable, with thick cushions covered in pretty flowery cretonne. Again, she suspected, the work of Thelma Ryman. The coffee was as good as Agnes remembered it. Polly ran about enjoying the new scene, new smells.

Thelma was very flattering about Brighstone Manor Hotel, then she asked about Tracey's card, obviously wanting appreciation to be shown towards Tracey and her thoughtfulness.

'Oh, yes, a pretty little card thanking me and regretting her previous invitation to Denise's. Very appropriate, Thelma, thank you.'

Agnes went no further. She wondered what the fond mother would think if she knew the truth, knew what her daughter was really up to.

'Isn't it unusual for a fourteen-year-old to be so thoughtful, don't you think, Agnes? I feel so proud of the way she behaves – but I expect I'm boring?'

Agnes made the usual reassuring noises and then could not resist asking if they had heard anything on the night the police had decided the murder had taken place, according to the pathologist.

'Nothing. Absolutely nothing. If you remember on that night we had that rainstorm. I got up about half-past one and went into Tracey's room – she had her window open nearly always and the rain would be coming in and soaking the carpet underneath the window. I must admit she never does anything about her window. Sleeps through it, as the young do.'

Agnes felt her heart give a lurch. Was Tracey in by then?

'I closed the window and Tracey just woke up for a moment, then turned over and went to sleep again. I think she did say thank you.'

Lucky Tracey, she must have just managed to get in, in time to leap into bed, show her mother she was there. Agnes remembered the rain pouring down after she had got back to the hotel with Polly. A near thing for Tracey, a very near thing. Was that when Tracey had managed to smuggle in the case of 'her gear' as she called it? Agnes thought not because she remembered telling her to run straight home. The case must have been retrieved the next day.

Thelma wanted to talk about the crime but was understanding about the way the conversation in the bar last night had steered away from it. She did mention the poodle who had eaten the dish full of nuts, laughing as she did so.

'It was such a lovely evening, Agnes, and did a lot to take away the nasty taste of that poor man being stabbed to death so close to us.'

The visit was pleasant but Agnes learnt little more about the girl who interested her. Only one thing her mother volunteered shed a little light on Tracey: she had few friends except the one she was staying with and Denise did not even go to the same school. She was two years older than Tracey, and both her parents worked – what they did for a living was not mentioned. They had only met Denise once and Richard thought her too loud and affected. But Tracey spent a lot of time with her, was very fond of her.

'But then he doesn't really understand modern girls. Tracey is such an exception, so reliable and trouble-free, he

73

can't fathom Denise. I expect she is all right. Anyway, Tracey will be good for her.'

'Little does the poor woman know her own daughter,' Agnes said to herself as her hostess went to the kitchen to make a second cup of coffee.

The conversation then reverted to the murder, how it could have happened and what the motive was. Thelma had lots of ideas which Agnes felt were mostly planted by her husband, Richard. She knew the dead man was a porter at the hotel and was interested to hear that he had parked Agnes's car for her when she arrived.

'When will Tracey be coming back, Thelma?'

Thelma obviously didn't know. Her husband felt it would be better if she remained at the friend's house in Newport while the police were still milling about on the hill. Well, Agnes thought, it really didn't matter. All she had to do was wait to see if the girl would demand something more. She was sure she would, and probably soon.

Agnes left soon after her second cup of coffee. As she walked down the hill, Polly on her lead let out to its fullest extent, she relived the moment of the killing. She wondered whether rescuing the girl had been worth it. The initial amount Tracey had asked for was not much, but what if she started asking for money for drugs? Would she perhaps start pushing to get more clothes, more make-up – Tracey was equal to someone much older than her fourteen years. How long had she been able to deceive, make fools of her parents, live the life she wanted to live? Agnes wondered if the brother, Jeremy, was a carbon copy of his sister. She felt she would like to get to know him.

Chapter Eight

'Oh, do come, Agnes, it's just a fork supper, salad and cold meats and salmon, you know; after a Sunday lunch a light meal in the evening is all you need really, isn't it?'

Thelma sounded as if she wanted Agnes to join them. It was two days after they had had coffee together.

'We will all be here. Tracey is here for the day at any rate. Jeremy is back too, and Richard is not going to the golf club for a change, so you will have the joy of meeting the whole family. If it is a joy, that is.' Thelma laughed as she made this little joke, using the word 'joy' in obvious quotation marks.

Agnes felt she would like to try and assess Tracey's attitude to her after the delivery of the card by her mother at the dinner party. She should have received the tights by now. Would there be any requests for anything else? Also she would be interested to meet Jeremy, who didn't appear to be the family's pride and joy. Indeed, he had hardly been mentioned.

'That would be nice – about seven thirty, Thelma?'

'Yes, lovely. Look forward to seeing you – we all are. Just jeans or any old relaxing clothes. We may take the food into the garden so wear flat shoes and bring Polly. Jeremy wants to meet Polly.'

Agnes agreed to all this with the exception of taking Polly, who wasn't the best of dinner or evening guests. She normally started looking for her accustomed bed at about ten thirty. She didn't mention this to Thelma, but just let it ride and would leave Polly in the hotel. This would also provide a good excuse to get away earlier if she wanted to or found herself bored with the whole proceedings.

Sunday evening Agnes changed from the dress she had been wearing for Sunday lunch and put on a denim trouser suit she felt would be suitable for a meal in the garden, or any occasion when one wanted to look informal and not 'dressed up'. The evening was fine and warm. Agnes set out to walk up the hill at about twenty past seven, full of curiosity about her meeting with Tracey and quite looking forward to seeing Jeremy, who had been painted, at least by his mother, as a bit of a waster. She was looking forward to seeing the brother and sister together and trying to understand why they appeared to be so utterly different.

Richard Ryman opened the front door and Thelma emerged from the kitchen. Both were very welcoming and Thelma finished drying her hands on a tea towel, looking embarrassed as she did so.

'Oh, no Polly, Agnes? What a shame!'

Agnes did her best to explain that Polly was not awfully good at evening parties, liking to cuddle up in bed at a fairly early hour. They walked into the sitting room, Thelma leaving the cloth on the hall table.

'This is my son, Jeremy, Agnes.'

The boy unfolded himself from the settee and greeted Agnes with a raised hand and a really enchanting smile. He was a handsome youngster – at least six feet and very slender. His hair, fair and curling on to his thin shoulders, added to his good looks rather than detracting from them. As he sat down again, he put up a hand and ran it through his hair. He looked slightly shy.

'Prefer to be called Jerry, Mrs Turner, if you don't mind.'

His lips curled in a half smile. He bore absolutely no resemblance to his sister, or to his parents. Agnes suddenly noticed that he was smoking. He crushed the cigarette out in a glass ashtray balanced on the edge of the sofa's arm;

it still smoked a little, the smoke rising straight up in the still air.

'Smoking in the house, Jerry, you know what I think about that.'

'Sorry, Ma. I forgot and lit up. I usually go into the garden.'

He slanted his long, thin body toward the ashtray and had a more successful go at stubbing the cigarette out. He gave a grin towards Agnes and she did her best not to return the smile. Here was a young man, she thought, who was highly endowed with the maximum amount of charm. He seemed to take after neither of his parents.

Tracey suddenly appeared. She had been in the garden 'practising tennis', she said. She looked hot and sweaty, although she had on cut-down jeans and a white cotton top. Agnes looked down the garden and saw a rotating umbrella-like structure, the tennis ball captive on a nylon cord hanging down from the wire above it. It was no longer rotating. Agnes met Tracey's gaze – it registered nothing.

'Oh, hello, Mrs Turner, sorry I'm so sweaty. I'll go and have a shower. I didn't realize it was so late.'

She moved across the room and at the door she turned round, smiled again: 'Looking forward to having a talk, Mrs Turner. Won't be long.'

Perhaps Agnes did detect a conspiratorial look in the girl's eyes – then she turned away and mounted the stairs leaving Agnes wondering just what she was thinking.

Richard served drinks, carrying the glasses in on a tray. Jerry had gone to the kitchen and was now back on the sofa swigging from a bottle of beer.

'My son prefers to drink in that disgusting way.'

Richard's comment showed more hostility, Agnes thought, than was strictly necessary, but perhaps the relationship was built on hostility.

'Saves washing up, doesn't it, Ma?' Jerry smiled good-humouredly, winked at Agnes and took another swig at the bottle.

77

They, or rather Richard, decided to eat in the garden. Out just beyond the french window was an attractive garden set, six chairs dotted around a table – the seats and backs of the chairs were cushioned by a blue and white patterned cover, slightly padded, that made them more comfortable than the cast-iron type that Agnes always found to be very uncomfortable. The drinks were taken outside, the evening was warm. Richard helped carry out the food but Thelma did most of the carrying and Jerry none at all. Tracey did not appear until everything was taken into the garden, then apologized for not helping and gave her father a quick kiss on the cheek, which made him smile, pat her on the arm and tell her not to worry, there had been enough people to do the carrying without her. At this, Jerry, lounging in a garden chair, tipping a bottle to his mouth at frequent intervals, gave Agnes a small, ironic smile and cast his eyes heavenwards.

Tracey was wearing a demure blue sleeveless frock, the hem well below her knees and the neck encircled by a white collar. The dress made her look like a very young nurse. That Tracey owned such a dress rather surprised Agnes, but perhaps it was a purchase made when she had been out shopping with her mother. She was charming to Agnes and asked her during the meal if she had walked from the hotel. When Agnes answered, yes, she had, she looked at her in feigned amazement and fright.

'Well, weren't you worried about the murderer – after all, they haven't caught anyone yet, have they? Daddy won't even let me go out there, will you, Daddy?'

Richard agreed with his daughter and turned to Agnes: 'No, and I will certainly drive you back to the hotel, Agnes.'

Agnes was very definite in her refusal to allow this and have the car out just to take her home. Jeremy suddenly spoke up in between his sips from the bottle, laughing a little, showing all his charm.

'I shall walk Agnes back and I shall personally demolish any murderer we happen to meet.'

Tracey broke in with an even louder giggle and a mean-ingful look at Agnes, not at all friendly.

'Oh, I think you can both be pretty sure you won't meet the murderer, don't you agree, Agnes?'

Agnes chose to ignore this remark. Tracey's father appeared to take exception to his daughter's treating the matter so lightly. His eyebrows drew together in a frown.

'He certainly hasn't been caught, Tracey, and may be anywhere. I admit it's not likely he would stay around here, but one cannot be too careful.'

Tracey was quiet after that, but cast one or two pointed glances at Agnes during the meal and now and again looked as if she was suppressing a titter. However, she made no attempt to say anything to Agnes during the moments they were left alone.

It was a very pleasant evening, the food was very appro-priate for the warm weather, the garden was beautifully kept – Agnes wondered how much of the beauty and order was due to Thelma rather than anyone else in the family. Agnes could not remember if she had ever noticed a gardener working there when she had visited. At last, after coffee in the sitting room, Agnes made Polly her excuse for leaving, although it was only ten thirty and Thelma begged her to stay a little longer. Agnes was determined, however, and shrugged on her jacket, and although she assured him she was not in the least nervous, Jeremy was not put off his determination to walk her home.

During the conversation while they were eating, Agnes had learned that Tracey was being taken to school the next morning by Richard and had arranged to stay another few days with Denise. Their studying was going so well, they worked so well together apparently, that Denise, who was an only child, did much better at school during Tracey's visits and her parents encouraged the relationship. Agnes privately thought this a trifle odd, but kept the thought to herself as both Richard and Thelma seemed happy with the arrangement.

'Come and see me again soon, won't you, Agnes?'

Always Thelma's parting remark, Agnes thought, but she promised she would do so and Thelma kissed her cheek at the front door and stood there until they had progressed a little way down the hill, Jeremy slouching along beside her. For a few yards he did not say a word, but whistled to himself tunelessly and pulled a leaf off here and there as he passed. At last he spoke, glancing sideways at Agnes.

'I'm glad you and Ma hit it off, Agnes.'

Agnes was not expecting such a remark and for a moment did not know quite how to reply. Then: 'Yes, Jerry, I have grown quite fond of your mother, although we have only known each other a short time. She seems a little lonely sometimes, I think.'

The boy took a handful of ivy as he passed a tree. He pulled it away, broke it off as if to underline his words, make them more effective.

'You can say that again, Agnes, very lonely. Dad's not what one would call a sensitive type.'

Agnes sensed a bitterness in the boy's reaction, and the verbal hostility she had noticed between father and son during the evening had intrigued her. She pressed the young man a little further and he seemed pleased to let out his feelings. Apparently Thelma had loved living in London and had been sad, very sad to leave, but when her mother had vacated the house and it had become theirs, right at the time of his retirement, Richard had insisted that the family move down to the Island. Thelma had disliked leaving her friends and London, was almost frightened of the move.

'She had lots of friends there, Agnes, it was her life, you know. She belonged to a book club, was on the committee of the Red Cross, the RSPCA. She led a busy and enjoyable life. All gone now, of course.'

Jeremy was obviously on his mother's side but Agnes could see the sense in Richard's move. As an accountant, retired, the gift of a house and the extra income from letting the house in London must have been tempting. She said as much to Jeremy, who disagreed hotly. His reply was that his father had already got friends on the Island because of his golf playing when they came down to stay with their grandmother, who seemed a great favourite.

'Dad joined the golf club down here the moment we moved. What did poor old Mum have to join? She doesn't play golf.'

Agnes refrained from comment, she certainly did not want to take sides in a family disagreement, but she did find herself divided in her opinion. She changed the subject and enquired about Tracey's reaction to the move. Jeremy laughed out loud at this.

'Oh, Tracey, she's learning to be a con lady, Agnes. That girl can turn any situation to her own advantage and come out smelling of roses.'

They had reached the manor and went through the gates. Agnes motioned towards the teak seat near the front door on the lawn. Jeremy draped himself on the seat in a way Agnes was getting used to. His accusation about Tracey interested her and she was determined to find out more.

'What do you mean about Tracey being a "con lady"?'

'Well, how did you think she was the perfect scholar in London – top in all the subjects before she left? Daddy's clever little girl.'

'Well, how did she manage to be so bright?'

Jeremy seemed delighted to spill out anything about his family. Maybe at twenty he had bottled it all up for too long, travelled around too long as well, but he seemed to Agnes to be genuinely on his mother's side. 'Ma', as he called her.

He went on to tell a few home truths about his sister. At the convent she had caught two nuns kissing and embracing – things nuns definitely shouldn't do. Jeremy made it sound amusing, but Agnes realized it must have involved a lot of anxiety and suffering for those two poor creatures. She had confronted them with what she had seen, but she wouldn't tell anyone, she promised, if they would let her have the list of questions and the answers for the mock exams. They had agreed and had done so.

'You can imagine why Tracey came top of the pile, head of the class, the brightest pupil ever.'

Agnes, thinking of her own position, was appalled. Jeremy still treated the matter as a joke.

'God knows what she's up to at the moment with this friend Denise – of course, because of the murder Dad feels she is safer in Newport than here.'

'I'll go and fetch Polly, Jerry, then perhaps you will take a little walk with her and me in case the killer is still on the prowl. All right?'

He agreed and Agnes went up to her room to fetch Polly. Jerry was stretched out on the seat when she came downstairs. The boy doesn't sit, she thought, he just sprawls, legs stretched out in front of him, hands linked on his chest. He got up and joined Agnes, bending down first to have a word with the little dog, rubbing her back in a way Polly particularly liked.

Agnes could not forget the story about the two nuns and his sister's involvement with them. If she could act like that, blackmailing was second nature to her. The thought made Agnes wonder just how far Tracey would press her case and how she should deal with it.

She wondered why Tracey had not mentioned the subject this evening, but they had hardly been alone together. She could, of course, have passed a note to her for Agnes to read when she got home tonight, but there had been no note, no demand. Agnes had absolutely no doubt that another demand for something would follow. Perhaps she should have reported what she had done to the police at once, but even then she could have been accused of manslaughter – only 'reasonable violence' was allowed even when a rapist was apprehended by a rescuer.

As the walk progressed round the garden of the manor, Agnes heard all Jeremy's ambitions and dreams. He wanted to paint, he believed he was quite good, but at

82

home his paintings were received with little or no interest. He sounded young, sad and frustrated, also very angry.

Agnes listened and sympathized, but her real interest was Tracey. She wanted to know more about the girl's motives. Jeremy did let one remark out that gave her cause to think: Denise's father owned a chemist shop in Newport and another in Shanklin. Would this, Agnes wondered, have any bearing on the close friendship between Denise and Tracey? Ecstasy, Agnes was sure, was part of Tracey's intake, when she went to the clubs with the boyfriend Agnes had seen her embracing at the bus stop. Maybe she was on something else too, something stronger? Heroin, crack cocaine, or maybe just amphetamines, tranquillizers – anything she could get. Could they be stealing from the chemist?

They came back to the big gates and the boy took his leave of Agnes. She was quite sorry to see him go and said so, feeling he needed support.

'I hope we meet again soon, Jeremy.'

'Thanks, it's been nice to talk to you, Agnes. And do go and see Ma often, won't you – she so likes you and she is a bit cut off.'

Agnes watched him head for the hill again to make his way home. A nice young man, she thought. Perhaps his painting was just a youthful dream, but perhaps he had a real talent? Anyway, he was not getting much encouragement. She watched him out of sight then walked back to the hotel with Polly. The young man stayed in her thoughts for some time.

Chapter Nine

Agnes walked slowly up the path to the front door of the manor, Polly trotting beside her and stopping occasionally to investigate an interesting smell on the grass edge or on the surface of the path itself. The hall was only lit by two shaded lights on the low coffee tables. Agnes was startled when a man's voice said, 'Goodnight, Mrs Turner.' It was the night porter seated behind the reception desk, half hidden. Agnes replied, mounted the stairs and let herself into her room, locking the door behind her.

Later, sitting at the dressing table taking off her make-up, she could not get the things Jeremy had told her out of her mind, particularly the horrible, heartless story about the two nuns. He had added that Tracey had been very gleeful when she heard that the younger nun had abandoned her vocation and left the convent.

For some reason which Agnes did not quite understand, the fact that she was not the first person Tracey had tried her blackmailing skills on, comforted her a little: the nuns, maybe girls at the school? Had these skills proved productive, had the girl gone from strength to strength? It was as if she, while still young, just a teenager, was practising hard to be an accomplished criminal and would become more and more expert as she grew older and more experienced.

When at last Agnes was in bed with Polly stretched out on her blanket, she found she could not drop off to sleep as she usually did. Nothing had come yet in the way of a further demand from Tracey but she had little doubt that it would. Suddenly she thought of Jeremy's suggestion that she might like to come and see his paintings one day. Agnes felt she would like to see them – the boy did not seem to be getting any support from his family. Maybe his becoming a painter, supporting himself through his work, was only a dream. Agnes felt she was not competent to criticize or judge if they were good or bad, only if she liked or disliked them; not, perhaps, very useful. At the moment all praise and admiration seemed to be centred on Tracey, Tracey who knew how to manipulate the people around her, get out of them what she wanted. Agnes resolved that Tracey must be stopped and maybe she was the one who could stop her. She looked across at Polly, who raised her head, brown eyes sleepy.

'We will see to it, Polly, won't we? After all, we always do, don't we?' Polly's eyes closed and her head fell back on the blanket. She began to snore. Agnes turned on to her side, pulled the pillow into a more comfortable position and very soon went to sleep.

Next morning Thelma answered Agnes's telephone call but when Agnes suggested calling round in an hour or two she explained that she had an appointment with the hairdresser at a quarter to eleven.

'Oh, Agnes, you know how much I love to see you. Can't you possibly make it tomorrow?'

When Agnes told her that she was really coming to see Jeremy's paintings at his invitation, she sounded astonished.

'Oh, did he tell you about his paintings? He doesn't normally talk about them to anyone, not often even to us.'

Agnes assured her that he had asked her and that she was looking forward to seeing his work.

'Richard gets so cross about Jeremy wanting to be a painter, says he'd probably make a great deal more money if he went into painting and decorating. He doesn't think he's got any talent at all.'

Agnes thought this was a pretty insensitive remark, but then she had not thought Richard Ryman a particularly sensitive man, especially where his family were concerned – the exception being his beloved daughter.

'Well, Jeremy seems to want to show them to me, Thelma, but I'd love to come and have coffee the next day if you will have me. I just can't resist your coffee.'

This remark seemed to please Thelma and she thanked Agnes for taking an interest in her son's 'hobby', as she called it. Agnes resisted the temptation to reply that she thought it was very nice of Jeremy to offer to show her his paintings.

'I'll look forward to seeing you tomorrow, Agnes. Please bring Polly.'

Thelma handed the phone to her son, who spoke rather shyly in reply to Agnes's suggestion that she would like to drop in and see him this morning.

'Hope you'll think my daubs are worth looking at, Mrs Turner. See you about eleven then?'

At about a quarter to eleven Agnes set off up the hill with Polly. She was rather pleased that Thelma would not be there – she realized the family were not close to their son's dreams and ambitions. Perhaps he was no painter, perhaps Richard had the knowledge to recognize that there was no real talent there and that accountancy was a much safer bet. Anyway, as she drew nearer the house her interest in seeing the paintings and drawings grew. Thelma's car was not in the driveway. Jeremy opened the door for her and led her through into the sitting room. On the settee was a large black portfolio, which Agnes guessed contained some or all of his present work. He picked it up as they entered the room and turned to Agnes, again rather shyly.

'Perhaps we could look at my work outside – the light is really more suitable there.'

Agnes agreed and Jeremy carried the case outside and placed it on the garden table. Agnes sat down in one of the garden chairs. Jeremy was about to sit down when he

86

suddenly remembered something and turned towards the house again.

'Oh, sorry, I forgot the coffee. I'll fetch it.'

Agnes sat and waited, not touching or opening the portfolio without her host there. After a few moments Jeremy came back carrying two steaming cups giving off the same delicious smell as his mother's brew. Agnes guessed she must have made it and left it in the heated coffee machine. Agnes sipped it with enjoyment. Jeremy ignored his for the moment.

'They are not much, just scenes that grabbed my attention at the time. Sometimes I think I've done something quite good, then I look at it again later and I think I'm useless, not got the scene at all.'

Agnes, having finished her coffee, gave her complete attention to the many and varied pictures. To her surprise several of them were portraits, head and shoulders: old men, their faces wrinkled and pockmarked; old women and younger ones; children, even a baby clutched in its mother's arms. The colours were good, and many of the pictures were of Indian children. Agnes remembered that Thelma had told her that Jeremy was or had been in India.

'I like them. I'm no expert, as I said, but they seem to me to be full of life and atmosphere.'

It was as if she had opened the door for the boy to voice his faith in his art. Agnes did not stint her praise, she felt that he got little enough from his family. At last he packed his work away. She asked him about his friends. They talked quite a long time about his future, whether he would ever be able to earn a living as an artist.

'I should be more like Tracey. She's tougher than me. She's really a tough cookie, that one. If I was like that I would get a larger allowance; more money would help, I can tell you.'

Agnes was curious about the remark and asked him what he meant, why he thought Tracey was so favoured and spoilt by her father? The questions opened a torrent from the boy.

'My sister Tracey is a little blackmailer, Agnes – she has been since she was twelve.'

The story he blurted out had a strange and horrible familiarity to Agnes. Wasn't she going through the same experience from the same girl? It was almost unbelievable anyone so young could be a serial blackmailer. Apparently, when she was twelve she had surprised her father in bed with his mistress, his secretary.

'But how did he allow his daughter to catch him in such a situation? Was he in his own house or did she see him somewhere else?'

As he told the story, Jeremy's tone varied from grudging admiration to disgust. The story underlined, at least in his mind, the fact that his sister was denied nothing she asked for, while he, who admittedly would not go the way his parents wanted, had his ambitions and dreams ignored.

'But tell me, at twelve, how did this happen?'

'Oh, as usual everything fell into place for Tracey.'

His voice was full of bitterness and frustration. 'It was in London. Ma came down here because Granny wasn't very well. It was a Friday. Tracey was at school and Dad was going to call for her and drive her home about five. At lunchtime she didn't feel well so one of the nuns drove her home. There was Dad, all nicely set up, in bed with this Myra Hayter – what a name! My sensible, wily sister never told a soul. Dad was right up the creek and after that, anything Tracey wants Tracey gets. She told me one day, not long ago. What could I do? I couldn't, wouldn't hurt Ma, so I just keep quiet. You are the only person I have ever told. Maybe I shouldn't have.'

Agnes shook her head and put a hand over his. She felt sorry for the boy faced with such a decision.

'Don't worry, I won't say a word. I wouldn't want to hurt Thelma either. I've got quite fond of your mother.'

Jeremy looked at her, his eyes warm and friendly.

'Yes, I'm glad. Ma's lonely – and do you know what frightens me, really scares me, Agnes?'

Agnes shook her head, guessing what he was about to say but saying nothing.

'That one day Tracey, my dear, loving little sister, might decide to use the knowledge she has about her father to Ma. Why, I can't imagine; she just scares me, that's all. I think Tracey's too wily to give away any secret that will be useful to her.'

He carefully did up the clasp on the portfolio. Agnes was curious about his last remark: she wondered whatever would make Tracey decide to tell her mother about Richard's escapade. She asked Jeremy.

'Well, suppose one day her father refused to give her something she decided she must have, would she in a fury decide to tell Ma? It would break her heart, even if it all happened years ago. Ma's the faithful type.'

Agnes understood his fear, and some of it transferred to herself. Supposing she should refuse any future demand Tracey might make, would Tracey tire of the game and decide to go and tell the truth to the police? Agnes did not like the risk at all.

The subject was changed. Jeremy confided to Agnes his next ambition was to go to China and paint and draw, but at the moment he was doing a job in London in a big hotel.

'I'm an underwaiter – very "under", I can tell you – but it's not too bad. I quite like it and it gives me a bit of time to paint in the early mornings.'

Agnes wondered if he told his parents about the life he lived to try and realize his dreams, but he shook his head and told Agnes rather sadly that he had at first, but they showed no interest and his father's answer was usually 'Get a proper job for goodness' sake, and stop bumming around, Jerry.' So he gave up. He had sold one or two paintings but he didn't even mention this to his family. Agnes had really enjoyed being with the young man, seeing his work. She had not enjoyed hearing about the shortcomings of Tracey. She felt a shiver of horror that a youngster of twelve had embarked upon the criminal activity of blackmailing. She was a bright scholar and could obviously have kept up without threatening those poor, stupid nuns.

Whatever admiration Agnes had felt for a teenager, creeping out at night, deceiving her parents in order to lead the kind of life she wanted, now melted away. There was nothing to admire in the way the girl behaved. Also she felt more apprehension about her own situation. It would have to be resolved.

Agnes thanked Jeremy for showing her his paintings and drawings. She really had enjoyed seeing them and had been agreeably surprised at the artistry and passion they showed. Polly was collected from her exploration and enjoyment of the garden – she loved new places, new smells. He walked with her to the front gate.

'Thank you, Agnes, it's been great having someone to talk to, and do come and see Ma tomorrow, won't you? She'll be looking forward to it.'

Agnes promised him she would not forget. It was nearly lunchtime and she decided to have lunch at the manor. She wondered as she walked back if there would be any further communication from Tracey. After what she had heard from Jeremy she felt his sister would surely not stop at asking for four pairs of tights. The fact that she had received them without protest would maybe encourage her to ask for something more, something most costly. However, when Agnes arrived back at the hotel there was no post or anything from Tracey Ryman.

Agnes had a light lunch, then telephoned Amy to say she had decided to stay on the Island for a third week. She had already made a longer visit than she had intended, but she felt herself growing fonder and fonder of the Island. Could she bring her little zoo of neglected and unwanted animals to the Island? She thought not. Amy might like to remain in charge of the Sanctuary. Anyway, Agnes was a long way from making up her mind one way or the other.

The Manor Hotel was a relaxing place, she rather enjoyed the meals put in front of her without any effort on her part to dream up the menus, or do the washing up and clearing away afterwards. Perhaps one day, when she was a good deal older, she would like to move into a rather superior hotel, have everything done for her. Anyway, for the present she was enjoying herself and the spice of danger and intrigue was doing a lot to take away boredom and dissipate the threat she always felt of encroaching depression.

The more Agnes thought about what she was beginning to call the Ryman Situation, the more she was puzzled as well as surprised that Tracey had confided in her brother about her ability to make things happen by becoming a blackmailer. Why tell him about the nuns? Why tell him about her knowledge of her father's infidelity – should she have kept this to herself? But perhaps she was unable to resist the urge to show him how clever she was, how she could get what she wanted, particularly from her father, when he, Jerry, could not even manage to get a decent allowance. Agnes thought she was perhaps beginning to understand the girl a little more. Criminals often gave themselves away, telling all, even in prison, when there was an urge to boast about what they had done, the money they had stolen, the fire they had started, even the murder they had committed. Certainly that could be the reason. Just a wish to show off the power she had, pride in what she was able to do. Agnes wondered about the friend Denise, who Tracey seemed so happy to be with, to stay with. Had both girls got a hold over each set of parents? Nothing, it seemed, was impossible where the wily, quick-witted Tracey was concerned.

The next morning Agnes kept her promise and walked up the hill with Polly to have a cup of coffee with Thelma Ryman. Thelma greeted her very warmly. She had bought Polly a present, a red ball, a big one, too big for Polly to get in her mouth. Polly started at once to push it round the

91

garden. Thelma watched her and said she looked like a footballer.

'Thank you, Thelma, that's really sweet of you.'

Agnes meant what she said and said it with real affection, but she wondered how much her feeling of affection was influenced by the fact that she knew Thelma was being deceived by all her family. Her husband, because of his infidelity, the daughter who was now profiting by his actions, and the son who knew the truth but was afraid to hurt her with it.

Certainly the Ryman Situation was a strange one and now she herself was part of it. There was certainly a great difference between her situation and theirs: she could stop hers when she wished. No one could threaten her without the inevitable reprisal. How and when this reprisal would happen, she could not yet say. Tracey obviously thought that blackmail was an easy way to get what she wanted. How could she know she had blackmailed one person too many? Tracey was unaware of the danger in the game she was now playing, but the danger was there just waiting to erupt.

Thelma seemed to be summoning up her courage before she managed to ask an important question.

'What did you think of Jerry's paintings, Agnes? Richard will hardly look at them. I can't give an opinion – I don't know enough about art and I usually don't like to contradict my husband. He wants Jerry to get a proper position in his old firm but Jerry won't even consider it.'

Agnes felt irritated by her friend. She couldn't understand how Thelma could side with Richard whilst not giving the paintings a real and unbiased judgement. After all, anyone with eyes could see that some of the portraits were outstanding. She said as much to Thelma, who hardly reacted.

'Portraits? I don't think I remember portraits. I only leafed through them, you know, Agnes. Richard was with me, with us, at the time, you know.'

Agnes understood only too well. Poor Jeremy. He seemed to have no chance to get taken seriously.

'Well, I think he's good and deserves some support, Thelma, really I do. Painting is his life, you know.'

Her hostess looked uncomfortable and made the excuse that she would get another cup of coffee. She left the room. Agnes felt she had made little or no difference to how Thelma felt about her son's 'hobby', either from her own point of view or from her husband's. In a way, Agnes wished she had said nothing. She determined to drop the subject completely and managed to do so when Thelma returned from the kitchen with the second cup of coffee. They switched the conversation to clothes, shopping and food. Agnes was soon bored and felt in a way she was letting Jeremy down by not supporting him and his work more. Not that Thelma could do much, but influenced by Agnes, she might have put in a word or two of support for their son's potential in the art world to Richard, who could perhaps increase the boy's allowance or do something constructive for him.

After the second cup of coffee Agnes called Polly, collected her new present, thanked Thelma and prepared to depart. She was a little surprised when, just as she was closing the gate, Thelma, who always came down the path to the gate, suddenly put out a hand and placed it lightly on her arm. Looking embarrassed, she said softly, 'You're right, Agnes, I should have taken more notice and been more interested in his pictures. It's Tracey, I suppose. She seems to get most of our attention. Richard is so proud of his daughter, I think if she asked for the moon he would try and get it for her. I suppose he spoils her.'

Agnes shrugged her shoulders and smiled. She felt there was nothing she could say at the moment to help Jeremy's cause.

'I suppose there are always favourites, Thelma. Fathers often favour and spoil their daughters.'

Agnes patted Thelma's hand and turned away for her walk home. If only she knew, she thought, how would she react, what would she do? Leave him? But she didn't know, and meanwhile her beloved daughter was reaping the proceeds. As she walked down the hill, Agnes decided that the Ryman Situation left her feeling rather dirty. Nobody in the family came out of this well – Tracey, Richard, Jeremy – only Thelma was innocent, unaware of the intrigue, deceit and nastiness that was going on all around her. But surely Thelma could be a bit more assertive, not take everything lying down.

Agnes walked into the Manor Hotel and went straight into the bar with Polly. She ordered a brandy with ginger ale – she really needed something to take the taste of the Rymans and their behaviour out of her mouth.

While Agnes was sitting sipping her drink, she couldn't help wondering again why Tracey had told her brother about her behaviour to the nuns and to her father. And what would the odds be that she might tell him about her own encounter with the would-be rapist and what she had done to him? If so, how would Jeremy cope with such a revelation? Keep it as secret as the rest? After all, he might think murder was more serious than the other episodes. Agnes tried to dismiss the matter from her mind. So much of Tracey's freedom and ability to leave the house at night, when she wished to, depended on her silence. Perhaps she would not let her brother into that much more dangerous secret.

Agnes finished her drink. Suddenly she did not feel like lunch, an indication that she was worried, well, slightly worried that such a complication might happen. Tracey – was she a boastful girl, wanting to show how much more clever and more daring she was than other girls? Was that why she had told Jeremy about her exploits in the London convent and the one-upmanship she had over their father? The nuns, after all, were no longer of use to her. Her father was well in hand. Telling her brother would do nothing to jeopardize that secret. Agnes felt the secret of the murdered man was safe as long as it brought in money, or whatever else she asked for. But maybe not for long. Agnes thought action must be hurried a little.

Chapter Ten

That afternoon Agnes was going to Ryde to call in a shop she had used a lot when she had lived on the Island. The manageress still remembered her many purchases and, indeed, a sort of Christmas card friendship existed between them. A few days ago Agnes had taken her trouser suit there to ask a favour of her manageress friend, Ella Dakin. Agnes wanted the sleeves of the jacket slightly shortened and the cuffs on the trousers taken away. This morning she had had a telephone call from Ella to say the alterations had been done and she could call for the suit any time convenient to her.

She set off after forcing herself to eat a light lunch. The afternoon was sunny but not as warm as one would expect at this time of year, cool enough to make Agnes think she would be glad to get her suit back. It was light but warmer than a dress, and formal enough to wear in the evening to the bar and dining room. Polly had been walked and was lying fall length on the back seat of the car. As Agnes set off she had, luckily, no suspicion that anyone was following her: the yellow moped behind her meant nothing to her. She had no suspicion of what would happen when she arrived at her destination, other than picking up her suit and paying for the alterations.

The large dress shop was empty of any customers when Agnes walked in. Ella Dakin was standing behind the main glass counter, and through the glass a selection of pretty and colourful headscarves gleamed silkily. Agnes was always tempted by silky headscarves but today she resisted. Ella looked up with a smile of pleasure when she recognized her erstwhile customer.

'Agnes, how nice to see you again. How are you enjoying being on the Island?'

Agnes smiled back and leaned forward to give her friend a quick peck on her cheek.

'I'm trying to resist getting another house here. I do enjoy being on the Island, it's so much more relaxing than the mainland. Maybe it isn't really so, maybe it's just me exaggerating.'

Ella Dakin pulled a face at her and laughed. 'Try managing a large dress shop like this one, Agnes, not very relaxing!'

Ella went through the curtains at the back of the counter and came out with Agnes's suit enclosed in a plastic see-through cover. She held it up and told her customer the price charged.

'Want to try it on, Agnes, and check that the alterations are all right? We shortened both garments to your measurements.'

Agnes shook her head and reached over to take the suit from Ella, when a voice behind her made her turn round, startled. Standing there was Tracey Ryman. She had not heard the girl come in or walk across to the counter. She had on a smart, black leather, short fitted coat, the ticket still hanging from the collar button.

'It would look so nice on you, Mrs Turner.' She slipped it off and handed it to Agnes. 'Go on, try it, I know you ought to have it.'

Very much against her will Agnes tried the coat on. Ella Dakin looked surprised, but pleased.

'You two know each other? Tracey's mother is one of my very best customers. Mrs Ryman, you know?' She looked at the coat a little uncertainly. 'Yes, I think it is rather you, Agnes, not your usual kind of jacket, but it does something for you.'

Agnes shrugged her shoulders; her eyes did not leave Tracey's face. There was no escaping the girl's meaning.

97

She wanted the coat for herself. If she didn't get it, what would she do? Go straight to the police and tell them everything? Agnes thought not. Kill the goose that was laying the golden eggs? She decided it was not the time to test her.

'Very well, I'll have it. How much is it, Ella?'

'A hundred and sixty pounds, and really worth it, Agnes. It's made by one of the best firms in the business. I buy from them when I want something special.'

Agnes handed the coat over to Ella and sat down at the small table next to the counter to make out her cheque. Tracey stood and watched her. As she handed over the cheque, Tracey spoke.

'I'm so glad you bought it, Mrs Turner, you'll never regret it. I'm sure you won't.' This was said with a slight sarcastic smile.

Agnes said goodbye to Ella and walked out of the shop, Tracey close behind her, Agnes carrying the two rather ornately decorated carriers. Out in the street when they were well away from the shop, Tracey held out her hand.

'Nice of you to buy me the coat, Mrs Turner – well, it was a bit young for you, wasn't it, and there wasn't much else you could do, was there?'

She took the bag and walked away. A bus drew up almost beside her. She turned round, raised the hand holding the coat and boarded the bus. Agnes stood for a moment and watched the bus drive away. She felt *her* lips curve in a little smile. She was suddenly sure of the path she was about to take, relaxed and certain of herself.

'So young too, but I'm afraid it can't be helped,' she murmured softly.

Swinging her other parcel on her fingers, she made her way towards her car. Polly danced about, pleased to see her. Agnes sat for a moment in the car, still smiling a little.

Agnes motored home, walked Polly then returned to her room, took off her shoes and stretched out on the bed. She was tired and felt the need to get her thoughts straightened out. There were many times in her life when she had reached this kind of impasse and then a good, long assessment by herself alone had always made her come to a sensible conclusion. She opened the new book that she was enjoying but threw it to one side, linked her hands behind her head and gazed at the sunlight on the ceiling. Polly decided it must be bedtime and jumped up beside her. Agnes gave herself up entirely to her thoughts.

Tracey and the nuns drifted into her mind. Should she take the trouble to go to London? She knew the name of the convent and roughly where it was. She could tell the Mother Superior how Tracey had blackmailed the young nun to give her the examination questions and even scribble the answers for her – but what good would it do? It would not get the young nun her vocation back, or help her in any way.

Then Agnes's thoughts turned to Richard Ryman. What could be done there? If she made Richard tell his wife about his affair, that he had taken his secretary to bed while Thelma was away looking after her mother, that would probably break her heart, maybe break up the marriage, and to add the fact that her beloved daughter had used her knowledge about her father to get whatever she wanted from him – what further harm and hurt would that cause poor Thelma?

All that and probably more. Doubtless Tracey had been blackmailing others – perhaps other schoolgirls. Then Agnes turned to her own case. How to handle that – murder, perhaps manslaughter; rescue from rape? How would that go down? When Tracey was safe at home in bed, her own mother giving her the perfect alibi – 'She was in bed when I went in to shut her window because of the rain coming in' – no, no use at all. Agnes picked up her book and resumed her reading. But she could not push the problem out of her mind.

The words on the page meant little or nothing to her. The girl dominated her thoughts – she was a truly evil creature. The leather coat – how would Tracey explain this expensive addition to her wardrobe to her mother? Perhaps she would not wear it home, but leave it at Denise's house. It would be interesting to see how she handled that recent new item. Agnes had to admit the thing had been skilfully done. The yellow moped she had seen once or twice – had that been driven by Denise? Did she know why her friend had wanted 'Mrs Turner' followed? Tracey had caught the bus back to Newport, so maybe, and perhaps more likely, she had not taken her friend Denise into her confidence. But then, how would she explain the coat? Well, Agnes would wait and see. She concentrated on her book and this time managed to get lost in it.

The next morning, Polly walked and fed, Agnes was just finishing her breakfast and studying a trio of brochures that one of the estate agents she had consulted had sent her. One in Seaview was rather intriguing. When Agnes had been living on the Island it had been an antique shop: now the photograph showed it had been turned into a rather cute little house in the High Street. Agnes had always been attracted to Seaview. True, a large estate had been built near, but the village itself remained fairly unchanged. A few shops, a couple of hotels and restaurants made up the community of mostly elderly people. She was just making up her mind to go and look at it when the waitress came to her table to tell her that she was wanted on the telephone. It was Thelma Ryman, sounding rather upset, and almost begging Agnes to come and see her, this morning if she could, as she was very anxious to talk to her about her daughter.

'I can't talk over the phone, Agnes, please come.'

Agnes decided at once that all the estate agents could wait and she would go and see what was upsetting her friend so much. See the house this afternoon perhaps.

'Is Tracey home, then, from her friend's I mean?'

Thelma sounded as if she didn't really want to talk

100

about this on the telephone, but she confirmed that Richard had fetched Tracey yesterday evening because Tracey had rung him and said she was bored with Denise and wanted to come home.

'He, of course, drove off at once to get her. She has only to crook her little finger and he goes running off to do what she wants. He spoils her, Agnes.'

Agnes listened with sympathy. If only Thelma knew what sent him running off to do whatever Tracey demanded – how shattered she would be.

'Please come – and bring Polly. Tracey's going to school and Richard is playing golf all morning, so I can talk to you and see what you think, Agnes.'

Agnes agreed to get to her house about a quarter to eleven. She would use the hill for Polly's walk, which she knew would delight her little dog.

Thelma greeted Agnes with her normal kiss and warmth. To Agnes's surprise, she heard voices in the background – it was Tracey and her father. He seemed in no hurry to get off and was sitting reading the paper. Also to her surprise, Agnes saw the leather jacket of yesterday draped over the back of the settee. Richard greeted Agnes.

'We're off in a bit, Agnes, so we will leave you two to chat in peace. Tracey's got a free period. That's why we are a little later than usual.'

Tracey crossed the room, smiling at Agnes, and picked up the coat, smoothing it with her hand.

'Isn't it cool, Mrs Turner, a present from Denise. Well, she had it for a birthday present and didn't like it. I think it's lovely, don't you?'

She slipped on the jacket and twisted around to show Agnes, who did not give an opinion, merely looked the girl levelly in the eye. Her look was returned without a shade of embarrassment.

'Want to try it on? It would suit you, it doesn't matter how old you are – this gear is OK.'

'Tactfully put.' Richard folded the paper and threw it on

101

to a chair and prepared to leave. 'Come on, Tracey, we must go or you'll be late for your next session of learning to live.'

Tracey smirked at him and put the coat back on the settee, picked up a satchel of books and made for the door. Even in her school uniform, Agnes had to admit she looked older than her fourteen years.

''Bye, Ma, 'bye, Mrs Turner, 'bye, Polly – see ya.'

She and her father disappeared through the door. Thelma stood quite still for a moment until she heard the slam of the car doors, then she relaxed.

'I'll go and get coffee, it's all ready.'

She went towards the kitchen. Agnes saw she was very near to tears and wondered whether it was because of the wretched leather coat – but why should that trouble her? After all, according to Tracey, it had been given to her as a present – did that matter so much?

Thelma came back with the tray, placed it on the coffee table between them and sat down opposite her guest. She looked very pale and terribly upset.

'They don't know – I mean Richard or Tracey don't know what I found, Agnes, I didn't mention it. I didn't want to tell them until I had talked to you.'

She stopped to put Agnes's cup in front of her and the plate of biscuits near by. Agnes felt Thelma was playing for time, trying to put off whatever it was she wished to talk about. At last she made up her mind.

'Agnes, you saw that coat, the leather coat. Well, obviously it was an expensive item – goodness knows why Denise didn't like it and, of course, Tracey wouldn't tell an untruth, would she?'

Of course not, Agnes thought, full of sarcasm unspoken.

'Anyway, she had it on when she came home last night – yesterday evening. Richard remarked on the jacket, but he only praised it and said if Denise was silly enough to give it away, well that was her problem. I didn't agree. They both laughed at me over what Richard called my "scruples". Thought I was silly.'

'Well, in a way they were right, weren't they, Thelma? I mean Denise wanted to give it away. Why not?' Agnes sipped the – as usual – delicious coffee and waited for her friend to justify her anxiety over the jacket. But Thelma was not silenced.

'Oh, it wasn't the jacket, Agnes, though I didn't agree with giving such an expensive thing away. It was something I found in the pocket.'

Thelma got up; she had not even sipped her coffee. She went round to the sofa table, opened the drawer and took something out, came round and handed a little packet to Agnes. Full of curiosity, Agnes opened the little coloured cardboard container – a pack of white pills, about twenty, mixed up with a further ten or so blue ones, in a small plastic bag. Agnes lifted that out and underneath was a syringe, under that a small pack of what looked like new needles. Agnes was silent for a moment, then looked up. She felt completely baffled and surprised by Thelma's find.

'Who do these belong to, do you think, Thelma? Denise or Tracey, and where did they get the drugs?'

Thelma broke down completely then, weeping.

'Oh, I don't know, I don't know, Agnes. I've told no one but you. I don't know what the pills are. Tracey would never, never use drugs. She wouldn't dream of doing such a thing – that I am sure of. It must be Denise, mustn't it, Agnes? Of course it must be Denise, but what do I do?'

Agnes looked for quite a few seconds at the contents of the little box, before closing it and very carefully placing it on the table in front of her. The sight of the box and what it contained sickened her. After inspecting what was inside she had packed back the contents just as carefully as she handled the box. First, the small card on which were fixed, under a stiff plastic cover, four needles, obviously new, each one covered with its tiny tube, also of plastic. But this, unlike the cover that kept them fastened on to the card, was opaque, white, hiding them. She had laid the syringe on top of this card; then the small see-through plastic bag containing the pills. Agnes remembered reading some-where or seeing a description of Ecstasy – it came in the form of pale blue or white pills. This she placed on top, hiding the syringe.

How many times in her nursing years had a syringe like that, or similar to it, been part of her day, part of her work. To be used legitimately to administer morphia, insulin, anti-tetanus compounds to relieve pain, to protect the patient against infection and hazards to life. Here, though, this syringe made her visualize something quite different. She could almost see it drawing up liquid from a hot spoon, not to make the patient feel better, or to ease pain. This syringe was to be used for quite a different reason: to disorientate, to destroy reason, to promote a short-lived sense of euphoria or well-being, to create dreams and sensations that, when they disappeared, left the recipient 'down', longing for the next dose. It made her sad.

'What do you think, Agnes, what can I do?' Thelma sounded in dire distress. 'That coat is worth a lot of money. You can see it's brand new, and what are those awful things doing in the pocket if it belongs to Tracey?'

The emotion, the anxiety, in her friend's voice shook Agnes out of her own thoughts.

'Thelma, if as we think, Denise gave Tracey the coat because she didn't like it or for some other reason, why did she leave that box of what they call "gear" in the pocket? Is it hers rather than Tracey's?'

Thelma looked down at the table, a finger tracing a pattern, her eyes reddening. Agnes could just hear her murmur: 'It must have been Denise's stuff, mustn't it? But why should Denise be allowed to give the coat away, it must have been bought for her by her mother, mustn't it? Surely they could have taken the coat back to the shop and asked for a credit note or something?'

Agnes agreed with Thelma, she had to. The truth about the coat would be a disaster for herself and for Tracey. What could she say to sidetrack Thelma? Her fear was that she would get in touch with Denise's mother and ask her

104

why she had let her daughter give away the leather coat to Tracey. Agnes thought she could put Thelma off asking too many questions – after all, she was used to doing what her husband or her children told her to do. Agnes did not think she had much determination to go her own way, but on this Agnes was wrong. Thelma did decide to telephone Denise's mother. Agnes was apprehensive as she watched her friend dial the number and sit down with the cordless telephone held in one hand that trembled slightly. The phone was answered promptly and Thelma began to speak, then cleared her throat to get rid of the huskiness that was probably due to nerves. She managed to begin the conversation.

'Oh, Mrs Hillier, I just wanted to thank you for having Tracey to stay with you. It was so kind, particularly a relief, too, after the horrid thing that happened here – the man getting killed.'

There was a pause as Mrs Hillier was no doubt saying something pleasant, then:

'Oh, Mrs Hillier, before I ring off may I ask you a rather personal question that I do hope will not offend you?'

Agnes felt the palms of her hands begin to dampen slightly. She drew a deep breath.

'The leather jacket that Denise gave to Tracey. It looked almost new and I am sure was expensive, very expensive. I do hope you didn't mind your daughter giving it away?'

The reply on the telephone was almost audible to Agnes, not the words, but just the excitable rise in the tone of voice.

'You haven't, Mrs Hillier? You know nothing about a leather jacket? But you must have – Denise gave it to Tracey, told her she didn't like it, said you . . .'

The voice at the other end of the wire went on for a few moments more, and then the receiver was put down. Thelma held her receiver for a moment before she put it down on the table, the little green light off. She turned to

Agnes, her face a picture of bewilderment. Mrs Hillier's reply had obviously upset her.

'Mrs Hillier says she knows absolutely nothing about any leather jacket, she certainly has not bought her daughter one. She has never owned such a garment. Agnes, Tracey wouldn't lie – what is going on?'

Agnes had been searching her mind for something to say that would not compromise herself or even Tracey. The coat she knew all about, only too well, but the drugs – who did they belong to? Who put them there? She tried to reply, to give some rational reply that would satisfy the girl's mother who, at that moment, burst into floods of tears.

'Thelma, you know how youngsters behave, they borrow each other's clothes constantly. Tracey has probably borrowed the jacket and asked Denise to say she had given it to her.'

This remark seemed to upset Thelma more than it comforted her.

'Tracey wouldn't do that, Agnes, she simply wouldn't. She never lies; I have never known her to tell me a lie, even a white lie. We have a relationship that has never needed untruths.'

Agnes could not help thinking about that 'truthful' daughter changing her clothes and meeting the boy, lying and cheating her family constantly, even blackmailing her own father. How mothers, and indeed, parents, have the wool pulled over their eyes, especially by a child as devious and quick-witted as Tracey. But it was the drugs that preoccupied Agnes. Who did they belong to? Who had put them there? Why hadn't Tracey removed them if she knew they were there? Such questions did not occur to Thelma, she just wanted them out of her sight. She obviously had a built-in horror of drugs and the thought that these were even remotely connected with her innocent, reliable and loving child was more than she could contemplate.

Agnes thought quickly. If she took the drugs away she just might be able to trace where they had come from, who

106

the pusher was. Ecstasy was pretty easy to obtain, Agnes was aware of that, but money would be needed. There were over twenty tablets there. Surely Tracey would miss them if she was aware of their presence. She made the suggestion to Thelma.

'Thelma, if you agree, I will take the drugs with me. Leave the jacket where Tracey put it, just thrown on the back of the settee – don't say anything about the drugs until I have found out where they came from. Do you agree to that?'

Thelma nodded. It was really no answer to any of her questions, but Agnes could see her one wish, above all others, was to get the drugs out of her house and not have to deal with them herself and to cut the association of them with her beloved Tracey. Agnes got up and carefully draped the coat as it had been when Tracey threw it down, then she picked up the little box, opened her handbag, popped the box inside and snapped the handbag shut, placing it beside her. Thelma gave a sigh of relief.

'Agnes, you are so wise about everything. I seem to have lots of family round me, but who can I tell? Not Richard, he wouldn't believe me, but if he did it would break his heart. Jeremy, well, he wouldn't bother one way or the other, he's so self-centred, and Tracey – well, I know she wouldn't do anything wrong, not if she knew it was wrong.'

Agnes felt she had had enough of Thelma, for the moment anyway. Jeremy and Tracey, the ones Thelma referred to as 'the children', were the only ones who knew exactly what was going on: the intrigue, the secrets, the deception, even the blackmailing. Agnes was still very well aware that she herself, although she knew so much of what was going on, was unable to tell the truth. Tracey had got the grown-ups totally silenced!

Agnes said she must go, collected Polly from the garden and put her on the lead. As she did so, her hostess came towards her and kissed her cheek. Agnes tried not to draw back, she felt she had done nothing but deceive Thelma. Not once had she been able to tell her the truth.

'What you said about teenagers borrowing each other's clothes . . .'

Thelma was walking down the garden path towards the gate as she told a little story that seemed to console her. Apparently during her schooldays in London Tracey had come home one weekend dressed in a denim jacket which was torn and not even clean and which she seemed to have changed for her own new denim jacket bought for her on her last birthday. Confronted with this, she had admitted the swap, but said she liked this one because it was faded and everyone wore faded denim now, not new-looking like her own. Thelma had been rather cross about it at the time – now it comforted her.

'There you are, just as I told you, Thelma!'

Agnes bade her goodbye and started down the hill. Polly, lead let out to its fall extent, ran around. The dog was so sensible, her wants so simple: walks, food, a game now and again, the grass, the wind and sun, even the rain, and fallen leaves. The thought of leaves reminded Agnes of the man's body sliding down the hill and she dismissed it quickly from her mind, returning to her analysis of Polly and, indeed, all animals. They were exploited, treated badly, and yet not one of them behaved as badly as humans. What animal would ever behave like this dreadful girl? Agnes's mind switched again as she reached the bottom of the hill and turned left towards the Manor Hotel. The drugs in her handbag, she must find out where they came from, who owned them, when were they going to be used and where? The thought excited her. At least life was not dull at the moment, no boredom and most important, no depression. She shortened Polly's lead and made her way to the bar. She was beginning to enjoy her visits to the little bar, meeting people and chatting.

'Brandy and ginger ale, Polly,' she said. The barman repeated her order, smiling at the dog.

Agnes sat quietly at her own little table in the bar, Polly, well walked and contented, at her feet. No ideas came to her about the scene she had just left, the blackmailed jacket, the drugs, the anxious mother, the rather outraged Mrs Hillier. She was gazing abstractedly at the door of the bar when part of the answer dawned on her – or in a way, was suggested to her. A young man came into the bar, pulling at the Velcro fastener of his helmet. As he took it off he revealed himself to be a good-looking young blond man of about nineteen. He walked over to the bar, holding his helmet under his arm. The helmet – Agnes could not take her eyes from it. Why had she been so sure that the yellow moped which had followed her Porsche to Ryde had been driven by Denise? It could just as well have been a man, a young man, the boyfriend she had seen embracing Tracey at the bus stop. Was he aiding and abetting the blackmail scene or did he know very little – was he the source of the drugs, the pusher? A new start! Agnes felt stimulated – a new line to follow, a new clue, was she right? She went to the bar and ordered another brandy and ginger ale. She could not explain it to herself but she felt a need for a little celebration. It was slender enough, this clue that the young man had given her. Was Tracey in charge of the boyfriend or the boyfriend in charge of her? That would be a thrill to work out . . . She sipped her second brandy and ginger ale. Did he work on the Island, and if so, where? Detective work – that Agnes loved. Research she often called it. But one had to act more like a detective.

Chapter Eleven

The next morning Agnes woke feeling exhilarated. As she slipped on her jogging suit, snapped on Polly's leash, her mind was listing the questions she wanted answered. Who was the boyfriend, what was his name, his job? What did he represent, the drug pusher or receiver? Where did the drugs come from? What drugs were involved? Was Tracey a pusher – did she make money from selling drugs or just use them?

The contents of the little box pointed towards 'shooting up': the syringe, the needles. There was money in Ecstasy, not as much as there used to be, but still some. It was the fashionable 'take' at the clubs these days. She wondered how much the little packet she had in the box was worth, and who would have eventually profited: Tracey, or the as yet unnamed boy? Breakfast gave Agnes more time to think and she was quite startled when the waitress came back to her table and said loudly and obviously for the second time – Agnes had been so deep in her thoughts she had not heard the girl the first time:

'You are wanted on the telephone, Mrs Turner.'

Agnes immediately thought it was Thelma Ryman in a state, probably, about the leather coat and the drugs. She was wrong. On the other end of the telephone was Jeremy Ryman, sounding a little embarrassed. He had a very nice-sounding voice, low-pitched.

'Mrs Turner, I would like a talk with you, if you could spare the time. It is rather important or, believe me, I wouldn't bother you.'

Agnes agreed at once. There was so much she could ask the boy; perhaps he knew something about the boyfriend or his sister's way of life.

'Would you like to come here for coffee, Jeremy?' Then she had a rather better idea for their meeting, so amended her suggestion. 'Why not meet me at my car? We can drive up to Brading Down, walk Polly at the same time, and have a drink at the local. How would that be?'

Jeremy agreed at once and a time was fixed. He would be at Agnes's car at a quarter to eleven and they would motor up to the downs and have a drink at the pub.

'It will be nice to get away, Mrs Turner. Dad's on my back a bit and Ma is upset about something. Thank you for offering to meet me and listen.'

Agnes put the receiver down with a smile. The young man certainly had been frank about getting away from his family – as far as he could. Agnes felt a certain amount of sympathy and was quite looking forward to seeing Jeremy again. She had no idea what he wanted to talk to her about. She must remember to ask him if he knew the name and work place of Tracey's boyfriend – though, of course, he might be completely unaware she had one. Agnes had noticed during her previous chat with Jeremy that Tracey had told him quite a lot about her exploits. She had, indeed, boasted about them. Maybe she enjoyed impressing her brother with tales of what she felt to be her extreme cleverness and daring. Did she confide in Denise to the same extent? Agnes was pretty certain that Tracey would keep quiet about the murdered man. What she knew about Agnes was too big to waste on boastfulness. Telling any other person about how she had seen Agnes pick up the knife of the would-be rapist and plunge it into him, kill him, was worth too much to give away. 'Accessory to murder', 'keeping evidence from the police' – she could just imagine Tracey's response to those accusations: either she wasn't there, or she was too young to be prosecuted. Oh, yes! Agnes thought. Tracey would have all the angles well sorted out, she was sure of that.

111

Agnes arrived at the Porsche first. She installed Polly in her seat at the back and had just got into the driver's seat when Jeremy appeared. He ran down the last bit of the hill, round the corner and into the parking lot. Agnes thought he showed the agility and balance of a deer – he had youth on his side and he didn't even know how precious and short-lived it was.

'Lovely car, Mrs Turner, just what I would like!'

He smiled widely as he got into the passenger seat beside Agnes. He said hello to Polly, who was seated alertly on the passenger seat behind him. She stood up and gave him an enthusiastic tail wag. Jeremy laughed.

'Just the dog to frighten a car thief Mrs Turner!'

Agnes smiled back, but gave him a little warning: 'If she is alone in the car and anyone comes up and tries the door handle, she's not quite so friendly then. She's not a bad guard.'

Jeremy smiled, too, but Agnes noticed he seemed nervous. As they drove towards the downs he said little – just one or two admiring remarks about the car which, Agnes thought, were made to play for time and put off what he really wanted to talk about. However, she herself kept the conversation going about the hotel and the car and Polly. She felt he would probably start to unburden himself when they were out of the car and in the less restricted area of the downs. She was right.

Agnes parked in her normal place for Polly's walk. The sun shone warmly. Polly ran about, her nylon lead stretched out to its fullest extent.

'I can't let her off Jeremy, she's apt to take off over the horizon, not respond to calls, and the walk becomes a nightmare. I even took her to a dog trainer, but he gave up in the end, so this is the answer. Her youthful days were responsible for her rather erratic behaviour, I think. She was not always kindly treated.'

Agnes motioned to the blue spool in her hand and demonstrated how it could be shortened and lengthened. She could tell that Jeremy was too polite to interrupt her, but that he was longing to speak, so she walked a few paces without another word. At last the boy appeared to make up his mind.

'I'm worried about all the stuff I told you when you came to see my paintings. I mean, about my sister, Tracey, Mrs Turner.'

Agnes noticed that he had changed from calling her Agnes and it was now 'Mrs Turner'. She mentioned it and Jeremy blushed slightly.

'I felt it was a bit of a cheek. I seem to have, well, burdened you with so many of our family problems – perhaps you thought I was being too outspoken.'

Agnes assured him that she certainly had not thought it 'a cheek', as he put it, and would he mind reverting to 'Agnes' which was much more friendly. The boy seemed to relax a little and thanked her.

'What did you want to talk to me about, Jeremy? I have something to talk to you about, too.'

They resumed their walk, both feeling more comfortable, Agnes hoped, and ready to talk. It took a few seconds, Jeremy pacing along beside her, shortening his stride to match hers.

'I felt I had to talk to someone, Mrs Turner – Agnes. Tracey will get herself into all sorts of trouble. She seems not to bother at all who she hurts or whose life she turns into a misery. I can't think what makes her like this.'

Agnes waited for him to go on, to enlarge a bit on what he was saying, but he lapsed into silence again as if waiting for some comment from her. She tried:

'Tell me, Jeremy, has Tracey got a boyfriend?'

At the adamant reply from the boy – 'No, she hasn't, Agnes!' – she thought of the meeting of the girl and a boy or man at the bus stop and decided to press the matter further.

'Are you sure she hasn't? I know she's only just coming up to fifteen, but girls like Tracey –'

He interrupted her with a little laugh.

'Oh, she's got what could be called a boyfriend. She

113

talks about Douglas quite a lot to me, but, of course, not to Ma and Dad – she says he's gay. That's where she gets any drugs she wants – there never seems any lack of supply.'

'But how does he get them, Jeremy?'

'His partner works in a hospital and simply steals what he wants, I think. Tracey sells them to Denise or any other of her mates, I suppose. I don't ask. It's such a dangerous way to live I try not to think about it.'

Agnes had to steer the conversation very carefully, she was not sure how much Jeremy knew. Did he know of the slipping out at night, the change of clothing, the leather coat? Had his mother mentioned the box they had found in the coat pocket? She thought not. She hoped not.

'Didn't you say Denise's father was a chemist, or owned a chemist's shop? I thought perhaps that was where she –'

Jeremy interrupted her at once.

'Oh no. He's a financial adviser, not a chemist. He did own two chemist shops at one time, but I thought he had sold them.'

Agnes did not ask any more questions about Denise. Thelma had liked the fact that Denise was two years older than Tracey, or nearly two years older – Agnes couldn't quite remember, although she did wonder why they seemed so happy to let Tracey stay with her friend. Maybe she had put the usual pressure on her father and he, poor man, would not dare to cross her. What a terrible mess to be in, she thought. To be totally in the power of someone else and that it should be your own daughter, just for a silly, thoughtless action. Agnes could not but pity any man who had spawned such a child.

Agnes and Jeremy lunched at a little pub in Brading. The boy seemed to have lost a lot of his inhibitions. When asked about his sister's 'boy friend', he was quite out-going.

'I told you, Agnes, she calls him Douglas and he sounds a bit useless. Doesn't work as far as I can make out – he bought himself a moped, Tracey told me – very second hand. Maybe she bought it for him. Don't know if she's ever been on it with him.'

He took a long pull at his glass of beer with evident enjoyment. Agnes was careful not to reply. She must not show herself to be aware that she knew anything about the yellow moped – or the boy. She felt as if she was walking on very thin ice and was glad when he turned the conversation to his travels in India, his longing to go back there, and he talked, too, about Italy. He was a very interesting young man.

As they finished their lunch and got up to go, Agnes wondered should she perhaps mention that it might be a good idea to say nothing about the talk they had just had, but the boy forestalled her.

'If you don't mind, Agnes, I would rather not say anything about what I've told you today, or even let Ma or Dad or Tracey know we met. You never know which way her mind will jump.'

Agnes agreed at once, pleased that the caution had not come from her. A little walk with Polly and they got back into the car, and started the drive home.

On the whole she was pleased with the time she had spent. She enjoyed being with Jeremy: his dreams and ambitions were so different from those of his family – no wonder he wanted to get away, a long way away. That he appeared fond enough of his sister to worry about what would become of her was very much in his favour, Agnes thought. She seemed to care little enough about her brother.

So Mr Hillier, Denise's father, was not a chemist. The young, gay boy friend might be the supplier, getting the drugs from his partner who worked in the hospital. The gay boy friend had recently bought an old moped: the yellow moped that had followed her car to Ryde?

Agnes drew a long breath. She had learned a lot but as far as she knew she had divulged nothing. It had been rather difficult holding some information back from

115

Jeremy Ryman. She liked the boy, but felt she could not tell him many things. She had had to be so careful. She did not know how much Tracey's brother knew about his sister's escapades. She could not mention that dramatic night on the hill, Tracey's getting out at night and changing her clothes. She could not speak at all freely because she had no clear idea of just what Jeremy knew. It was like walking on eggshells. In some ways she felt rather mean, taking advantage of his knowledge but telling him very little of what she had found out. Agnes had enjoyed lunching with him and had been more relaxed talking about his ambitions, his dreams about his painting and his longing to travel all over the world, painting and sketching. He loved the car, his licence was in order and Agnes had let him drive part of the way home. They parted, however, outside the village just in case anyone saw them together, especially any of the Ryman family.

'Thanks, Agnes, it's been a help. I don't want Tracey to end up an addict. She's very self-willed and anything could happen to her. I do hope she is not as completely heartless as she seems.'

He walked away, a handsome, gifted young man, Agnes thought. She waved a hand from her car. He waved back, smiling. He had loved driving the Porsche, speeding a little at times.

Agnes felt tired, the guarded chatting, giving nothing away, was stressful. She gathered up her mail and she and Polly went upstairs to have a little siesta. This was getting to be a regular routine with Agnes and she wondered, as she took off her shoes and stretched out on the bed, if she was getting old. Polly jumped up beside her and snuggled down. Agnes opened her mail – some sent on from Amy, some from the local estate agent. She flicked open the folders, particulars of three houses: two were impossibly ugly, but the third was a pretty, fairly modern little house, surrounded by a beautifully tended garden. Three bedrooms, quite different from her present house. Alas, by the look of it, no room for poor Amy!

Agnes questioned herself: would she want to live on the Island again after her recent experiences? Murder, blackmail, drug-taking? Agnes felt it wouldn't put her off. She examined again the brochure of Elm Tree Cottage, a pretty name for a pretty house. She would go and look at it, perhaps tomorrow morning. The house was just outside Yarmouth with sea views – this was one of Agnes's favourite parts of the Island. The price quoted on the brochure was astronomical. Agnes felt quite complacent about her financial state – she could afford that and also buy the new Porsche. After a rather impoverished youth, it was nice now being comfortably off.

She got off the bed, had a quick shower and put on a dress suitable for dinner at the manor. She touched up her make-up, fed Polly – her walk would come after dinner. She decided she would take the little dog on a walk up the hill.

The dining room was fairly empty. Agnes was an early diner and not very hungry. She toyed with the starter, her mind fall of ideas: a visit to the hospital might be a good idea. Had Thelma lost her nerve yet and mentioned finding the drugs to her daughter? So much to think about, so much to find out. She finished dinner, skipping the dessert. Upstairs she slipped on a light coat, the evening felt colder. She snapped on Polly's extending leash and made her way downstairs.

'Just going for Polly's walk, Mrs Turner? I hope you don't get caught in the rain – it's been spitting a bit. Don't get caught in a downpour.'

The receptionist was just putting on her coat and the night receptionist was getting ready to take her place. Agnes smiled back at both of them and made for the front door. As she walked down the steps on to the path towards the big gates, she was pleased to find no rain falling. Anyway, Agnes thought, Polly had had several good walks today, she need not go far, just halfway up the hill would do, as far as the path that led down to the main road. She looked at her watch, twenty to nine, not likely to meet

anyone from the house on the hill. She knew the pro-
gramme of that house a little now. The lead let out as far
as it would go allowed Polly to go into the leaves and have
a little dig. Agnes paused by the path, looking down to
where she had seen Tracey meet the man she now knew
was called Douglas. She tried to remember what the boy
had looked like when he embraced Tracey. The street light
seemed slightly misty. Agnes stopped gazing down at the
road and her eyes wandered back to Polly, who was still
digging. As she watched her little dog, something higher
up caught her eye. The bus had just come round the corner
on the road below on a slight incline, causing the headlights to flash up amongst the trees. Something glittered,
just for a second, but long enough for Agnes to wonder
what it was. She stepped down two or three yards, carefully so as not to slip on the damp leaves. There was a hole
in the tree as if, some years ago perhaps, it had had a large
branch cut off from the trunk. Sticking out from the hole
was the tip of a blade which had picked up the light from
the bus's headlights. Agnes could reach it easily. With
finger and thumb she gently eased the blade out – there it
was! The knife she had used to kill Tracey's assailant. It
couldn't be any other. Agnes shivered.

The knife held in her hand, she remembered throwing it
away from her, thinking it had followed the body. But no,
perhaps it had ricocheted off one tree and virtually disappeared in this hollow or almost hollow tree. No wonder,
Agnes thought, the police searching the ground so dili-
gently had not found it. Only that little flash of light on the
end of the blade sticking out had made Agnes notice it. She
felt the wooden handle of the knife – it was quite dry,
the blade clean and bloodless. The rain had washed the
weapon clean. Agnes took off her headscarf, wrapped it
around the knife and put it in the pocket of her coat. She
felt very shaken by seeing the killer knife again. Agnes
reeled Polly's lead in and walked back up to the main part
of the hill. The rain started to come down, pattering on the
leaves of the trees around her and delighting Polly.

'Come on, Polly, time to go home now.'

Polly, on the shortened lead, ran in front of her down the hill, round the corner and up the drive to the front door of the manor, glad to get in, thinking of food.

'Just caught you, did it, Mrs Turner?'

The night porter was shutting the big hall windows against the rain, which was now coming down with a vengeance.

'I'm afraid it did, but not much harm done. It makes the grass smell so fresh, doesn't it?'

She crossed the hall to the stairs, shaking the raindrops out of her hair. Hairdresser tomorrow, she remembered, and gave no thought at all to the knife in her pocket, not for the moment, anyway.

Once in her room she took the knife out of her pocket and unwrapped it. In the room, away from the trees and darkness, it seemed to resume its normal character. It was just an ordinary kitchen knife – not intended to end a life, but nevertheless, it had. What to do with it? Agnes caressed the wooden handle and smoothed the blade. Then, carefully, she wrapped it up again in the headscarf, opened her cosmetic drawer and laid it behind the bottles and tubes. She felt the need to keep it safe, away from everyone. They – the police – had searched and searched for it, but she had found it. Fate of some kind had taken a hand, Agnes felt. Why, and what to eventually do with the weapon, she had no idea, but the feeling uppermost in her mind was *hide it, keep it safe*. The reason might suddenly dawn on her.

Agnes sat down at her dressing table and creamed her face, getting ready for bed. As she closed her cosmetic drawer she felt again that little shiver of fear – or was it delight? What strange twist of fate had made her find the knife, the very person who had used it?

Chapter Twelve

The next morning, just after breakfast, Agnes received an 'urgent' telephone call from Thelma Ryman. She sounded to Agnes as if she was in a state yet again. She couldn't, she said, talk on the telephone. Could Agnes come up to the house as soon as she could?

Agnes had planned to meet the estate agent and go with him to have a look over Elm Tree Cottage. She did say to Thelma that she had made some other arrangements for this morning. However, upon hearing this, Thelma became even more tearful or anxious. Agnes felt she must go and see her, so telephoned the estate agent's office and altered the appointment to the afternoon. Thelma was, as usual, profuse in her thanks and explanation. But Agnes was getting a bit irritated by what she felt was Thelma's inadequacy.

'Tracey's gone to school, Richard's gone to the bank and then he's going on to the club. I'll be alone here, Agnes, so I can tell you everything that happened. Jeremy's in bed, he usually gets up about twelve – not often before that. I don't want him to know anything, Agnes.'

Agnes made a little grimace at this last remark. She felt Jeremy knew far more about his sister than his father and mother knew about their daughter. What could have happened to cause Thelma to be so upset? Agnes couldn't quite imagine. The leather coat she supposed would cause more argument and explanation, but the real nub of the problem, Agnes could guess, was the drugs. Tracey would demand the box be returned to her or would deny all knowledge of the box, and make out Denise or somebody else had slipped it in her pocket – she knew nothing whatever about its contents. She would lie well and Thelma would believe her if it were possible and tell Agnes when she arrived that her daughter had never told an untruth to her in her life. Agnes went up to her room to fetch Polly, wishing in a way that she had missed Thelma's telephone call and had escaped to the estate agents before the plea came.

Agnes walked very slowly up the familiar hill, giving Polly plenty of time to dash about on the end of her long lead, investigating this and that. This was not entirely for Polly's enjoyment. Agnes was not looking forward to the meeting with Thelma. She felt it was fraught with danger; what could she say in answer to any questions Thelma might ask? Some she could answer with all innocence – just. *'I really have no idea, Thelma, no idea at all.'* That seemed to be the stock answer she must use. She knew so much that Tracey's mother had no suspicion of. As Agnes reached the house she comforted herself by thinking that Tracey would not give up any of the knowledge she possessed that gained her power over anyone else. The secrets that made her able to get what she wanted, go where she wanted, would surely be guarded and Agnes had, of necessity, to guard them as well.

Thelma's front door was wide open and she was standing there waiting, looking tearful. Agnes felt a twinge of irritation for a man and woman, Richard and Thelma, who could lose control of their fourteen-year-old daughter and, as far as Richard was concerned, absolutely through his own stupid fault. She hid the feeling and approached Thelma with a smile. Thelma reached out and took Agnes's hand and drew her into the house, almost as if she was afraid Agnes would change her mind and run away. In spite of Thelma's air of anxiety, she gave her usual enthusiastic greeting to Polly.

'Bless her, they are so uncomplicated and straightforward, aren't they, Agnes? All animals. I wish people were a good deal more like them!

They walked through to the sitting room. Agnes sat down and, as she did so, she saw again the shining black leather jacket flung unceremoniously over the back of the settee. The small box taken from the pocket was still in the handbag she held now, on her lap. Thelma continued to walk about the room as if she found it quite impossible to be still and sit, and say all she wanted to say.

'I'll go and make us some coffee, Agnes.'

Agnes stopped her determinedly and patted the seat beside her.

'Never mind the coffee, Thelma, we can have that later. Do come and sit down and tell me why you are so upset. What's happened now?'

Thelma at last lowered herself on to one of the arm-chairs, sitting just on the edge of the chair, not attempting to sit comfortably. She took a tissue from her pocket and Agnes thought the tears were going to start again. However Thelma made no movement towards wiping her eyes, but just pulled the tissue into small pieces and then screwed the whole thing into a little ball. Then, at last, she seemed able to tell Agnes what had happened:

'I lied to my daughter, Agnes. For the first time in her life I did not tell her the truth. I feel awful about it – lying to someone I'm so close to.'

Agnes turned in her seat and longed to reply to this with: '*How many times do you think she has lied to you?*' but, of course, she could not say that or the girl's deceptions would have come tumbling round their ears and Agnes had too much at stake to even think of saying such a thing. So she asked the question that she knew was safe and would reveal nothing.

'What did you lie to her about, Thelma, the drugs?'

Agnes felt if Thelma had told her daughter she hadn't found the drugs, she, Agnes, was pretty safe. What was dangerous was the girl's mother finding out about Tracey's various deceits and realizing that Agnes knew all about them. Her pulse quickened a little, but when Thelma answered her question, relief flooded over her. Only the mystery of the leather jacket and even more the little parcel of drugs had been lied about. And the lie had been a 'get-out' for Agnes. Thelma had denied all knowledge of finding the little box in the pocket of the jacket and had even gone so far as to say she had never touched it after Tracey had thrown it on the back of the sofa. If she denied all knowledge of the box, she couldn't know it contained drugs. Agnes hated feeling so vulnerable, but vulnerable she was. She was quick to praise Thelma.

'You did quite right, Thelma. What good would you have done to say you had found the drugs?'

'I don't know, Agnes, I really don't know. If she was found out what would happen to her?'

'She won't be. Denise may have given her the drugs or just put them in her pocket. We don't know, do we?'

Thelma perked up considerably after this remark. She looked relieved as if a huge weight had been lifted from her.

'Agnes, that fits in with Tracey's story. She told me Denise's father gave her the coat and made her promise not to tell her mother. He bought it for her as a present and Denise wore it once and didn't like it and gave it to Tracey. That's what Tracey said.'

Agnes was becoming more relieved as each part in the story was being revealed; she smiled.

'There you are then, Thelma. Denise had the drugs and that's how they got into the pocket of the leather jacket. Tracey really wasn't responsible for them being there. Luckily we found them and kept them, or at least I have kept them, so at least Tracey has got rid of a little cache of drugs she didn't know she had. So your lie has probably saved Tracey. Where Denise got the drugs, though, I intend to find out. Denise is a bad influence on Tracey, perhaps, but at the moment we must say nothing. Right? Tracey can be left innocent of the affair.'

Thelma at last relaxed a little and smiled too, as if in response to Agnes's optimism.

'Oh, Agnes, I knew you'd help. I'll say nothing, nothing at all, we never found the drugs.'

She got to her feet and came over to kiss Agnes on the cheek. The colour had come back a little into her cheeks and she made for the kitchen to prepare the inevitable coffee.

'I'm going to make coffee now, Agnes. You do deserve it. I am relieved, Tracey will be relieved, that we found nothing. That's all to the good. I'm still worried but not as much as before.'

Agnes sat waiting, many questions going through her mind. *'What box?'* She could just imagine how puzzled Tracey would be, hearing this from a mother who never, never lied to her. Even the fact that Mrs Turner had been there that morning would hardly make her doubt her mother. Things were 'on hold' at the moment, but even so the situation would require careful handling. Kid gloves were the order of the day, Agnes thought, with a wry smile.

Agnes stayed long enough to drink the coffee Thelma had made. Thelma's attitude had altered. She seemed to have accepted the advice – *no one saw a little box, no one saw any drugs.* Maybe it was the first lie she had ever told her daughter but obviously she was going to stand by what she had decided. Agnes left, having endured another kiss on the cheek. She decided that after she had lunched, seen the estate agent and the inside of Elm Tree Cottage, she would visit the hospital (someone might even remember her there – it was not all that long ago) and find out who Douglas managed to get drugs from. It was a long shot, but surely worth a try.

Although she was rather preoccupied after her visit to the house on the hill, Agnes gave her full attention to the estate agent's information and the tour round the cottage, which could have been called a house rather than a cottage. There were three bedrooms, four if you counted a tiny fourth room, beautifully decorated. Agnes had to admit the decor was to her taste and if she felt like moving here there would be literally nothing that needed altering or redecorating. The garden was incredible – back and front. If everything was perfect inside the house, the gardens were perhaps a little too perfect. Not a weed in sight and the flowers rather like little ranks of soldiers. Agnes asked the estate agent:

'How many gardeners did they employ?'

'None,' the agent replied, smiling. 'The lady did everything herself and though she has vacated the house she comes here every other day and works to keep everything as neat as you see it. Even cuts the lawns and puts in new plants, trims the shrubs.'

It was the one thing that put Agnes off. What about Polly? she wondered. She could demolish a neat and tidy flower bed in minutes unless watched. Agnes thanked the estate agent for coming and showing her over the property and said she would let him know after she had thought about it. She loved the part of the Island in which the house was situated – a totally different area from where she had lived before – but the garden had put her off. Letting it go and develop into a more natural surround seemed to be an impossible alternative to its present park-like look. She did not fancy having a gardener or maybe more than one gardener, doing a systematic change of flowers and planting them in such a regimental fashion. She came away from Yarmouth feeling the house was not for her. Disappointing, perhaps, but there it was – and she was not even sure she wanted to come back to the Island. She drove towards Newport. The hospital next – she would surely find great changes but there might be someone who would recognize her. It would have to be someone she could ask about drugs, whether they had any pilfering these days.

The visit to the hospital itself was not useful. She was allowed to wander about with no one, nurse or anyone else, asking what she wanted. The wards had been altered and the names on the entrance board changed so Agnes could not recognize them. The only Sister she thought might still be there and perhaps not yet retired was a Sister Taylor on the men's surgical ward. She found the ward at last, but was told that Sister Taylor had left about two months ago. Disappointed, she went back to her car which was parked in the visitors' area outside the front of the hospital. Before leaving she decided to drive round the back of the building to see if they had altered that as much as they had the front. Here she was luckier. She drove slowly past the part which used to be the maintenance buildings – this was where the maintenance engineer, overseer of the electricians, bricklayers, painters and dec- orators, had his office. He was quite an important boss in his little kingdom. He had been a middle-aged, grey- haired man when Agnes had worked at the hospital and she felt sure he would be retired by now. As she drove by, however, the green-painted gate opened on to the path and the very man she was remembering came out and glanced into her car. He stopped at once and his face broke into a smile. Pleasant as it had always been, his face looked a good deal older and there were wrinkles around his eyes and mouth that Agnes did not remember being there before. How we all age, she thought.

'Hello, Sister Carmichael, haven't seen you for ages!'

Luckily, Agnes remembered his name and gave him a quick smile of recognition. She had always liked him.

'Mr Wright, nice to see you again. It's been a long time, hasn't it? Have things changed?'

The man nodded, his face anything but happy.

'I tried to have a quick look round the hospital but I didn't get much further than the new big front hall. That's all very different.'

'No, it's not the place it was when you were here, Sister Carmichael, not the discipline there was. Nobody seems to care as much as they did. Too many computers and not enough TLC, that's what I think, but then I would, wouldn't I? I retire next month and I'm glad to go. Very glad to go.'

He laughed but his laugh sounded hollow and sad. He turned away as if he was about to go, but Agnes stopped him.

'Oh, we had a few hiccups, even in those days, Mr Wright. Do you remember when all those sheets disappeared and the surgical scissors, and the codeine tablets – there were one or two slip-ups.'

'Oh, yes, Sister, I remember the sheets. Two dozen pairs, wasn't it?'

'I expect things are a bit tighter here now, Mr Wright, or are there still amazing disappearances? Do you have a problem with drug pilfering?'

To her surprise Mr Wright clammed up and did not answer that question. Indeed, he pointedly avoided it by looking away and gave an evasive reply.

'Drugs? Not so you'd notice, Sister, but I expect there is always someone on the make, especially amongst the young ones with their clubs and their parties.' He laughed again, but shut his mouth firmly and would not make another remark about drugs. He looked admiringly at the car.

'Posh car, Sister.'

Agnes paused long enough to wish him a very happy retirement and, with a final wave, drove away. It had been nice to meet someone she knew, and someone who had often come to her rescue in Casualty and Outpatients when there had been an electrical crisis or other maintenance had been needed. But his retirement made her feel older – or, as she amended it as she drove along, 'more mature'. She pushed that thought firmly away.

When she arrived back at the manor there was a telephone message waiting for her from Jeremy Ryman. Would she ring him back as soon as she could? The message was accompanied by his mobile number. Agnes felt apprehensive. Jeremy's main cause was always protecting his mother. Tracey was pretty ruthless. Agnes wondered if the girl had threatened to tell her mother about her father, Richard's, little lapse. Jeremy was only too well aware what such an exposure would do to Thelma Ryman and Agnes felt he would do almost anything to protect her from knowledge that would break her heart. Then again it might be about that little box that disappeared . . .

Agnes went to her room and rang Jeremy's mobile number. He answered at once, sounding a little agitated. He asked could he walk down and have a word with her? Agnes replied, yes, come at once. It was drinks time and she felt she would have to forgo her usual changing for dinner and they could go to the sitting room and talk there. It was often deserted at this time as the hotel guests would be either primping up for the dining room or making for the bar. She had had a fairly adequate lunch so if the news Jeremy brought was something that needed talking through there would be no hurry.

Jeremy arrived promptly and they retired to the – as Agnes had expected – deserted sitting room. The boy had hardly sat down before he began to spill out what had happened. She had been quite right – the nub of all the trouble centred round the missing small box containing the syringe, needles and pills.

Apparently, Tracey had been furious when she discovered the coat pocket was empty and eventually she blamed Denise, who had tried the leather jacket on. Tracey, according to Ma, had flung out of the room and telephoned Denise, accusing her of taking whatever was in the pocket. Denise had been as furious as Tracey and the two had had a right royal row on the telephone.

'Agnes, you wouldn't have believed the things they said. Ma tried to stop it; she's easily upset, Ma.'

Agnes knew only too well what was coming next. 'Your mother told Tracey I had taken the box, did she?'

Jeremy nodded; he looked miserable and frightened. 'Tracey really lost it then. She accused Ma of shopping her, that she shouldn't have told you, or even let you see the box. There was a syringe in it, wasn't there, and some needles?'

Agnes nodded. 'That's right, Jeremy, and now she's aware that I have got the box, how is she taking that?'

A waiter looked in the door, questioningly at Agnes: 'Are you dining, madam?'

Agnes shook her head, no, she felt dinner was out and anyway, she didn't want any.

'Would you bring some beer and sandwiches and a brandy and ginger ale, is that possible?'

Agnes was rather a favourite of the waiter and he smiled and nodded at her and her guest. 'Will do, Mrs Turner,' he said.

'I don't know how your sister will react to this, Jeremy. Your mother has let the cat out of the bag. I wish she hadn't, we agreed to say nothing, but I can understand why she did. I think she is a bit frightened of her daughter, isn't she, Jeremy?'

He nodded. The sandwiches and drinks were brought in and nothing more was said about the box until Jeremy was leaving. Then he looked questioningly at Agnes, his eyes worried, his brow crinkled.

'What are you going to do about it, Agnes? I mean this could finish Tracey's school career, couldn't it?'

Agnes at that moment had not the faintest idea herself how she was going to handle it all. Tell, and it would involve her in Tracey's revenge – what would the girl do? She had a lot to answer for if everything was revealed. Accessory to murder, pushing drugs, being out at night when her parents thought she was safely in bed, underage drinking, sex. Yes, she had a lot to lose. Agnes waved goodbye to Jeremy, she felt both sorry for and irritated with Thelma. Why couldn't she have kept her mouth shut, kept her own counsel? Agnes would wait for Tracey's reaction. She had no idea what a terrible reaction and reprisal it would be. Something she had never dreamed could happen.

After Jeremy had gone, Agnes went to her room, collected Polly for her late evening walk. At the gates she turned right instead of left. She felt a real dislike of the wretched hill up to the house – so much seemed to be happening on that hill and in the house at the top. She felt contempt for the daughter of the house, who would exploit anything that moved. The father who hadn't the guts to tell his wife what he had done, perhaps in a mad moment, and beg forgiveness; Thelma, who couldn't keep her secret when frightened by Tracey. Even Jeremy, the member of the family she liked the best, appeared to have a weak streak in him. The wretched girl was running rings around all of them.

Polly tugged towards the hill, but Agnes would have none of it and walked determinedly the other way. As she walked she played with the idea of going home and leaving them all to sort themselves out, but such a way to resolve a problem was not in her nature. She had always sorted out things before walking away from them. Had she known what she would have to go through and suffer, well, perhaps she would have gone home. But even if she had, in a way she would still have been at the mercy of this girl, who she felt would stop at nothing to get whatever she wanted. Certainly the small piece of water between the Island and the mainland would not stop her.

No, Agnes felt she must stay here and put an end to the girl's blackmailing, find some way to silence her.

Chapter Thirteen

'There is a message for you, Mrs Turner.'

The day receptionist called out to Agnes as she was crossing the hall the next day with Polly beside her on a short lead. She crossed to the reception counter and took the white envelope handed to her. No stamp on it, just the written words in the middle: *Mrs Turner.*

'It was delivered by hand about half an hour ago.'

'Who delivered it, did you notice by any chance?'

The receptionist nodded and smiled at Agnes: 'Yes, I did. A young man. He didn't take his helmet off – seemed in a great hurry. He was on a yellow moped. Parked it at the bottom of the steps and roared away. Well, not very fast – it was an old bike.'

Agnes guessed at once it must be from Tracey Ryman. She moved away from the desk towards the front door, then stopped and took out the neatly folded piece of white writing paper. In the middle was a message, brief and very much to the point:

Mrs Turner, you owe me £100 for the Happy Pills. I do hope you enjoy them and they cheer you up a bit. Please put money in case – back in its usual place on the hill. Syringes and needles you may keep. Don't let me, or most of all, yourself down. It wouldn't pay. You do know what I mean, I am sure.

That was the end of the message – computer-written. Agnes folded the sheet of paper, put it back into the

131

envelope, pushed it carefully into the pocket of her cardigan and continued on her way to her car.

She got into the car with Polly and determinedly thrust the matter of the note from her mind. She did not want it to distract her from her driving and at the moment her mind was too full of it. When she reached the downs and was walking with Polly, the car safely parked, she would turn her mind on to the problem the note had presented to her and try and deal with it rationally: whether to pay or ignore.

What would Tracey do if she chose to withhold her reply and let it drift by her? As Agnes walked along she felt herself becoming more and more determined. She could not go on acceding to the girl's demands, giving her more and more. When would it stop? Never, as far as Agnes could see. If she said 'No more' and Tracey decided to tell all, she would be as deeply in trouble as Agnes – her involvement could be proved by Agnes herself. Could she say she had watched Tracey stab the man with the knife he had dropped, then had watched her run away, climb through the open window of her house? She would be an accessory then, but not a killer. No, Agnes rejected that idea. She felt she must rely on the fact that Tracey would not tell. The boy was involved, drugs, the hospital – Tracey would have to tell so much it would not be worth her while and maybe the blackmailing would have to stop. Agnes began to favour this idea. By the time Polly had had her walk, Agnes went and sat down on the teak seat that commanded a view of the south of the Isle of Wight to the sea which sparkled in the sunlight. As she sat there, Agnes felt more and more that she was right. The impudent request for the tights, then the leather coat, so cleverly got out of her, now a hundred pounds. No, no more. She would act as if the note had never been delivered.

On the drive home her decision did not change, indeed it grew stronger. If Agnes had had the slightest idea where this was going to lead, she certainly would have paid, without hesitation, the money asked. But she didn't know, so she stuck to it and when she arrived back at the hotel she screwed up the note and envelope and threw them in the waste basket.

In the afternoon Agnes took a chance and walked up the hill to where she had originally discovered the case where Tracey paused to change her clothes. There it was in its original place. Typical of the girl's daring, Agnes thought. Admittedly the police seemed to have withdrawn from that area, though they were constantly coming back to the place near the road where the body was found. Well, they would never find the weapon now, Agnes thought, with a good deal of satisfaction. She glanced up at the window of the Ryman house and thought she saw someone at the window. If it were Tracey she might be checking to see if Agnes was leaving the hundred pounds she had asked for. It was Saturday, she wouldn't be at school. Well, Agnes thought, she was going to be disappointed. As she thought this, Agnes did feel a slight tremor of apprehension. Tracey, although young, was not an enemy to be trifled with. Even this apprehension did not make her change her mind and she did not look up at the window again, but turned away and walked down the hill with Polly trotting at her side. She could imagine that upstairs in her bedroom Tracey was smiling to herself. Having seen Agnes approaching the case of clothes she would be under the mistaken impression that her victim was doing just as she wished and depositing the money as ordered in her note – and probably the pills as well. Agnes would hardly want them, Tracey was sure to think, nor would she want to be 'in possession of drugs' either.

Agnes would have loved to be able to stay and watch the girl's anger and disappointment when she discovered that Agnes had put nothing in the waiting case. But that was not possible, so she continued to walk down the hill and back to the manor. Wondering, too, what would be Tracey's next demand, for surely there would be one – that was how blackmailers work – and even taking into account her tender years, Tracey was clearly very quick to learn.

That night Agnes did not sleep well, indeed she couldn't sleep at all. Polly woke now and again and looked curiously at her mistress. Agnes knew that Tracey was aware by now that there was no money in the case – why wasn't she getting in touch? Agnes felt the girl would have no hesitation in telephoning her at any time, while she was out at some club or other, or when she was on the hill or at home, but the telephone did not ring and the failure of Tracey to get in touch worried Agnes and kept her from sleeping. By the morning, nothing. Agnes got up and put on her usual leisure suit to take Polly up to Pooh Corner, thinking no doubt she would hear from Tracey today, probably this morning. She was wondering if she should go out or stay in, and decided on the latter course. The lack of communication was beginning to make her doubt the wisdom of what she had done; she would stay in the hotel all day just in case Tracey telephoned or brought a threatening note. Whatever, Agnes felt she would like to confront the girl, really convince her that she was not going to get anything more out of her. There would be no more leather coats, certainly no money. Face to face that would be difficult, but might lead to some sensible conclusion. Polly must be walked but otherwise she would stay here and await events. It would be boring but necessary.

The morning was overcast and a few spots of rain greeted Agnes as she left the hall and went through the french doors into the back garden of the manor. The man with the two Labradors had come back with his wife for another weekend break and he was walking up the path towards Pooh Corner. He greeted Agnes as she passed her with his usual smile.

'Good morning, Mrs Turner. Not going to be a very nice day for us, I'm afraid, nasty dark skies and raining. Looks as if it's set in for some time.'

The two Labradors returned Polly's greeting with their usual sober dignity. The rather over-friendly Dobermann puppy gave an over-excited leap at Polly. His master restrained him firmly.

'Going to obedience classes now, Mrs Turner, and believe me, he needs them. Ate my slipper in the night and took the bottom off the wife's handbag during the week. He always apologizes, of course.'

The dog crowd who met at the weekends were a nice, friendly lot and up to now none of the dogs had picked any quarrels. Even in the bar the dogs sat around and minded their own business. The Dobermann pup was the only one who always wanted a 'gamey' and there was one rather unfriendly spaniel who looked belligerent. The lady with the white poodle had not appeared again, much to some of the men's disappointment! Her dog eating the dishful of nuts was still remembered.

The rain got a little heavier so Polly pulled her way over to the broken-down wooden structure which she always favoured when it was wet. Agnes gave in to her, letting a little more of the nylon lead out as she walked across the path which ran down the middle of the area. She let Polly have her own way, hoping she wouldn't take too long, as the rain was now coming down harder, and the sky was darker.

'Come on, Polly, hurry up! I'm getting soaked here.'

Agnes said this aloud and a woman leading a brown dog – what Agnes called a dog with a leg at each corner – smiled at her. She had not met the woman or dog before.

'A rescued chap; his first experience of a hotel stay. Rescued from the dogs' home. Can't make it all out yet.'

Agnes patted the dog's head as he passed her. He looked up, big brown eyes appealing – but a trifle puzzled. Polly was busy under the enclosure, turning round and round. Suddenly there was a commotion on the other side of the little field that made up Pooh Corner. The belligerent-looking spaniel, mistaking the Dobermann pup's invitation to play as an attack, started a fight. Agnes moved across to help. She placed the storage reel of Polly's lead on top of one of the posts holding up the little wooden structure – there was a hole in the middle of the reel of nylon and she anchored it by threading the hole over the large nail on the top of the post. Polly looked interested and would have liked to join in but Agnes didn't think that was a good idea, so she left Polly quite safely tethered, as she thought, and walked over to the fight. There was more noise than biting. The Dobermann had got hold of one of the spaniel's ears, and a small brown dog had joined in with much more serious intent. Agnes managed to get hold of that one by the collar and separate him from the others. In a few minutes the whole scramble was over, no real harm done and the various participants separated, their owners smiling, telling their dogs off and apologizing. Agnes backed off and made her way back to Polly.

There was no Polly, only the lead, and that had been cut through. Agnes picked up the end of the blue nylon; the cut across the nylon was obvious. The lead was very strong. Agnes's heart sank – standing there, she had no doubts this was Tracey's reprisal after finding no money in the case. It hadn't taken long. She felt herself crying in her head, 'Polly, Polly, where are you, what will she do to you?' Tracey had never shown any affection or even liking for the little dog the couple of times she had seen her. It must have been so quick, so quiet, Tracey surely couldn't have gone far? Agnes crashed her way through the rather dilapidated wooden palings into the field beyond, to left, to right – no one; opposite the side of the hill, no one. How could Tracey and Polly disappear like this? The rest of the dog crowd were taking their dogs back to the hotel, only the Dobermann's master noticed. He came over to Agnes, holding the offending puppy on a very short leash.

'Polly gone?' he asked.

Agnes nodded miserably, holding the nylon reel in her hand, looking all round the deserted field.

'Don't worry, she'll soon come back. Expect she's just having a run around on her own. Did the lead snap? They don't usually do that. I've had mine for years. They are made of nylon, you know.'

Agnes could not explain, so she smiled and said nothing. She was longing to leave there and start searching, but her heart was full of foreboding. Police, local people, the dogs' home at Bohemia Corner – where to ask? What to do? For a start, Agnes crossed and recrossed the field at the back of Pooh Corner calling, calling, 'Polly! Polly!' There was no response, no excited little creature dashing back to her across the green. Agnes knew that if the little dog could come in answer to her call, she would. But the cut nylon lead made her feel sure Tracey had taken her. Her hope was that the blackmailing girl would telephone soon and tell Agnes what she wanted for giving Polly back, or at least tell her where she was, where she was keeping her. Agnes now knew she would give the girl anything, anything she asked for as long as she would return Polly unharmed and quickly. Surely she would telephone soon, but when Agnes eventually returned to the manor, there was no call – nothing. She felt distraught.

At last, early next morning, having spent a sleepless night, Agnes called Thelma Ryman. She asked to speak to Tracey. Thelma, sounding a little puzzled at the request and still upset about the drugs, immediately started to ask about the pills and syringe. Agnes said she hadn't found out any more about them yet, but she would like to speak to Tracey.

'She's not in, Agnes. She spent the night at Denise's house – they have had a quarrel over the coat, silly pair. I can't make out what it's all about.'

Agnes did not tell Thelma that Polly was missing. She felt she could not even talk about it at the moment without breaking down. She didn't want to try and explain anything to Thelma Ryman. She rang off before Thelma made the normal request for her to come to coffee. She guessed that Tracey's mother must be shaken up over Tracey, but Agnes didn't want to talk about that either. She would go to the dogs' home and see if they had Polly. She had already been there once yesterday evening; they had been very pleasant and co-operative but, alas, no Polly. The police, too, had taken down the description of Polly and promised to telephone if they found her. Everyone was helpful, but could produce no Polly or even news of having seen her.

Agnes had no faith or optimism in these enquiries. She was almost certain Polly was shut up somewhere and couldn't get out, perhaps without food or water. The thought haunted her, she couldn't sleep, and her appetite was destroyed. When the hotel staff got to hear of Polly's disappearance they were all quite wonderful – as were one or two of the visitors who were familiar with Polly and fond of the little dog. Two of the waiters and one of the waitresses went out again and again, searching the fields round about, climbing the familiar hill Polly so liked to walk in, calling her name. Of course, Agnes could not tell them the full story. To them, Polly had snapped off her lead and run away and not come back. They mentioned once or twice the dangerous vicinity of the main road, and though they did not mention it, clearly thought Polly might have run that way and got knocked down by a car. Agnes could not agree with them, she felt something much more intentional than accidental had happened to the dog, her beloved Polly.

She tried again and again to get hold of Tracey, but she was always unavailable. Eventually, on the fourth day of Polly's disappearance, she telephoned Agnes. Tracey did not beat about the bush, she was clearly very sure of herself and knew, or thought she knew, she had Agnes at her mercy. The loss of her dog would bring her down, make her do anything she was told to do.

'Well, Mrs Turner, you've lost your little doggy, haven't you? Do you want her back, Mrs Turner? Naughty of you not to have left anything in the case. That would have made all the difference.'

Agnes felt her hand trembling so much she could hardly hold the receiver.

138

'Where is she, Tracey? What have you done with her? Has she got food and water? It's four days now. Please don't carry on with this – what do you want of me? You can have the money and the cardboard box. Please, Tracey, I want Polly back.'

Tracey laughed and was silent for half a minute, savouring her triumph.

'Oh, we are in a state, aren't we, Mrs Turner? I'll tell you what I want you to do. Put my little box of you know what and two hundred pounds in my case, which is in its usual place – you know that place – on Friday. I'll be coming home then. When you've done that I'll tell you where Polly is.'

Agnes hardly let her finish before she broke in: 'But that's two more days, Tracey. Please tell me now.'

The receiver was put down. Agnes dialled the number of the house on the hill but there was no reply. Agnes put her own phone down. She felt sick with anxiety, utterly vulnerable, and to make it worse, she could tell no one the truth about what was going on. No one. It was like being in solitary confinement, alone in a situation that must be kept strictly to herself. Two more days – that would be almost a week since Polly was taken. Was she being looked after, fed and given something to drink? Or just shut up somewhere and left to herself? If that was the case, the little dog would be frantic. She would put the money and the box of drugs in the case as Tracey had instructed – but two days away! Anyway, she would go on looking, she couldn't stop that. She would go to the bank and draw out the money today, at once. Perhaps if she put it there now, Tracey would come tomorrow morning and . . . no, it was no good. Tracey had said two days and Polly might have died in that time.

'Lunch is just going to be served, Mrs Turner. Won't you . . .?'

Agnes shook her head. After Tracey's call she could eat nothing. However, despite her feeling of distrust, Agnes drew the money from the bank. As she did so, she was crying in her heart: *'It will be too late, too late, why didn't she demand this before? It will be a week and Polly may be dead.'*

Thursday was a day Agnes was never, never to forget. After making herself eat some toast and drink a cup of coffee, she went out. Not in the car, she started walking around the field that looked on to the hotel behind Pooh Corner. She had searched the field and its surrounds time and time again. At the edges the field was surrounded by more copses, trees and shrubs, prickly bushes of blackberries. Agnes had forced her way through most of it during the last week, in between motoring around, looking, looking, calling, calling. The dreaded hill took up part of one side – the trees and a bare patch of land that looked as if, long ago, it had been a few allotments. Broken-down sheds still stood at the end, so decrepit that you could see right through them, their broken planks still just holding together. Agnes had searched through them several times, once in the pouring rain and again in the sunshine. She had felt hopeless as she looked at the wrecked little 'lean-togethers'. Now she paused and gazed round the field. From where she stood she could see the edge of Pooh Corner. Where was Polly now? Was she even alive? Agnes felt tears rising to her eyes. She wiped them away and tried to pull herself together. She stood for a moment. Birds were singing. How could they sound so cheerful when she was so sad?

Then she heard it. A scratching noise that was not like the trees scratching on the wood – it seemed to come from the second shed, or rather the skeleton of the shed. She forced her way through some rotting planks criss-crossed over what might once have been the door. The scratch came again. On what had been a bench stood a cupboard, almost covered with a rotting piece of tarpaulin. Agnes dragged off the tarpaulin to reveal a door. The scratch came again. The door had a hook on its frame and fitted into the hook was a latch. Agnes wrenched the latch off, losing half a nail as she did so, but she didn't even notice the pain as blood ran from her finger. For there, giving a little whimper as she saw Agnes, was Polly. She tried to get up but was too weak. However, she did manage a very feeble tail wag. Blood was coming from her mouth and she held up one paw which was also bleeding.

'Polly, Polly love, how could I have missed finding you?'

The inside of the box-like prison was soaking wet. Agnes gathered Polly up in her arms and started out to the hotel across the field. Tears were running down her cheeks. It seemed an age but actually was only minutes before she reached the manor. The receptionist saw her come in carrying the dog and she followed her up the stairs to her room.

'You've found her! I'm so glad, so glad, Mrs Turner. I'll get some warm milk for her.' She turned to go and Agnes called after her:

'Please do, and ring the vet, any vet you know, and ask him to come at once, would you?'

'Yes, of course. He only lives up the road – he may be at home today. I'll do it now.'

She went downstairs, back to the hall and her telephone. Within a few minutes one of the waiters arrived at the door with a little dish of warm milk – the receptionist must have told him Polly was found. Agnes put it near Polly's mouth: she drank the milk thirstily and tried to get up to do so, but couldn't so she settled to drink lying down. Agnes stroked her gently. Every rib showed on what had been her rather plump little body. Tracey had starved her. There was a rap on the door and the receptionist ushered in a tall, florid, heavily built man.

'This is Mr Campbell, the veterinary surgeon. He was luckily at home.'

'What have we got here, then? Mrs Turner, isn't it?'

He crossed over to Polly. Agnes explained that the little dog had been shut in a box for, as far as she could tell, five days. The vet had his stethoscope out and was listening to Polly's heart and lungs, taking her temperature. He was quick, gentle and efficient. Agnes liked him.

'She's very dehydrated. I'll put a drip up just for tonight. You'll have to watch her, see she doesn't take the drip out, as they do, Mrs Turner. All right?'

The drip was put in with the minimum of fuss. A little square of fur was shaved off and in went the needle, held in place by an adhesive plaster.

'Can she have anything to eat, Mr Campbell?'

The receptionist was back again, asking the question. The vet started to pack away his things in his bag. He patted Polly's head.

'Think she'll be all right, Mrs Turner, probably the rain-water kept her alive. As to food, she's been starved so go easy. She can have half a scrambled egg now, bread and milk – only a little before bedtime. As much water as she wants, but the drip will rehydrate her.'

He put on his coat and picked up his case. He turned back to Agnes.

'I'll call in tomorrow morning to see how she is. Food little and often, Mr Turner. Did someone shut her up, or what?'

The receptionist opened the door and accompanied him downstairs. Agnes watched them go: obviously they had met before. She heard the vet say as they went downstairs, 'What bastard could have imprisoned that little dog, my dear? Some bloody yob, no doubt.'

Agnes did not hear the woman's reply to him. She sat stroking Polly's head, her mouth drawn into a firm, thin line. She was no longer crying.

'Yes, Mr Campbell, a little bastard imprisoned that dear little dog and, by God, she's going to pay for it,' Agnes said quietly, almost to herself.

Agnes did not sleep at all that night. She lay beside Polly, watching the little dog as she slept soundly and snored a little. Every now and again Polly twitched a bit as if she was having a bad dream, perhaps about being shut up, starved, frightened, tearing at the door to try and get out. Agnes could not get over the fact that she hadn't heard her. Perhaps she had only searched while Polly, exhausted, had given up for a bit and gone to sleep. The vet said the rain, pouring into the prison the dog was in, could have helped keep her alive. She had lived on the puddles of rainwater. As she thought of it, Agnes felt herself shaking with rage. Had Tracey meant to leave her there until she died of hunger? Agnes thought so. The girl, Agnes thought, was completely heartless, without a trace of pity for anyone, much less for an animal belonging to a person whom she was blackmailing – from whom she was waiting for money, who knew too much for her comfort. Well, Polly was safe – Agnes hoped, recovering. But Tracey – she would be dealt with soon. Very soon, and without a trace of mercy.

Chapter Fourteen

The vet, Ian Campbell, arrived before breakfast the next morning. The first thing he did was to take out the needle from Polly's leg and remove the drip. Polly winced a little as he withdrew the needle. Agnes, thanks to her past experience in the nursing world, knew how very dangerous dehydration on such a scale is to both an animal and a human, and how much the drip could do, and had done, to counteract it.

Mr Campbell was pleased with the little dog's progress. Polly struggled to her feet, tail wagging to greet him. He stroked her head and she lay down on her blanket again, not quite the old lively Polly yet, not by a long way.

'I can examine her properly now, Mrs Turner. I didn't want to bother her too much yesterday, but she is so much better this morning. I want to see why she was bleeding from the mouth, if she has lost a tooth trying to bite her way out through the door.'

'She's limping quite a bit, too. And there's blood on her foot.'

He examined Polly's mouth and then her paw. Having her mouth looked at did not seem to bother Polly at all, even when the vet drew back her upper lip a little.

'No, teeth seem all there. Gums a bit torn and bloody, again because of her attempts to get out, biting the wood of the door.'

The foot was a different matter. The dog whimpered and drew the paw away as soon as he touched it.

'She's torn one claw right out, look – there's the hole it's

144

made. Painful, it must have hurt her when she pulled it out – again trying to escape.'

He held the paw gently in his hand to show Agnes the raw hole from which the claw had been torn.

'Never mind. It may not grow again, and it will hurt for a bit. The antibiotics in the drip will cope with any infection, and I've brought a little boot for her to wear for a day or two and some more antibiotics.'

As he talked and treated her little dog so very gently and kindly, Agnes began to realize more and more the trauma Polly had been through for almost a week. The hate in Agnes's heart grew and grew – what could repay such treatment? Tracey had clearly imprisoned the dog and never gone back to give her water or food. How could anyone behave like that? If Polly had died, and left a few days longer she might well have, Tracey could not have cared. She was incapable of caring about anyone or anything. She was torturing her father – yes, he had been in the wrong, but the completely heartless use of anyone's wrongdoing, even the nuns', was inhuman, without compassion. What kind of adult would she turn into?

Agnes had to switch her mind back from her thoughts of Tracey to listen and take in what the vet was saying. He was stroking Polly's thin ribs, each one standing out on her once well-covered little body. She turned on her back, loving the fuss being made of her, four legs in the air, getting more and more like the old Polly.

'She's young, she will soon recover, Mrs Turner. Take it slowly.'

He maybe sensed Agnes's preoccupation and put it down to the worry she had been feeling about her dog. At least, Agnes hoped he did. He would have been surprised and probably a little horrified if he had known her thoughts and in which direction they lay. *What kind of adult would she turn into?* No kind of adult if she could help it.

'Soft food for the moment because of her gum injury.'

He gave Agnes an encouraging smile and touched her hand.

'I'll see her on Monday, Mrs Turner, she can come to my surgery. You have a car, haven't you? Don't let her walk too far, especially on rough ground. All right? She will soon be her old self.'

Agnes nodded and thanked him, He handed her a card with the address and times of his surgery. It was in Newport.

'Just telephone my receptionist.'

He was gone, closing the door softly behind him. Agnes watched it shut, then just had to let go! She burst into floods of tears and put her arm around Polly. All the pent-up emotion of the last week welled up. Polly rolled over and licked her face. They were together again. Polly was safe.

After she had calmed down a little, Agnes telephoned Amy to give her the good news. She made it all sound like an accident. She could not, of course, tell the truth.

'I shall come home after the weekend if Polly is well enough, probably on Monday. If anything happens to stop me I will let you know at once.'

Today was Friday. This weekend might be the watershed. If all turned out as she hoped, she could go back to Sussex and Amy and put the Isle of Wight absolutely out of her plans. She would never, never forget what Tracey had put Polly through. The cruelty was terrible – and not only terrible but totally unforgivable and Agnes had absolutely no thought of forgiving.

Polly did look better now, though, and in spite of her sore gums and teeth she managed to get the little boot off her damaged paw and tear it into pieces. On her way carrying Polly down, taking her to Pooh Corner, Agnes had a word with the receptionist.

'I wonder, would you mind not letting too many people know that I have found Polly? The police are still looking for whoever took her.'

The receptionist was reassuring and told Agnes that the

changeover of 'weekend break' guests would be happening and the new ones would know nothing about the little dog. She would tell members of the staff, particularly the ones who had been so helpful, not to mention the fact that Polly had been missing and was now found. Agnes did this with a purpose in mind: Thelma Ryman would not know Polly was safely back, so in that case Tracey might not know.

Agnes decided to try letting Polly walk around a little on the grass, but the torn-out claw was obviously still painful and the little dog limped badly, even trying to go around on three legs which wasn't much of a success. When she visited the vet on Monday she would ask him for another boot and see this time that Polly didn't think it was a new toy and busy herself tearing it to pieces. Her ribs still showed her thinness and a couple of new guests with dogs who had arrived last night looked at her curiously. Agnes felt they probably might talk together and suggest the poor little dog wasn't getting enough to eat.

After Polly had breakfasted on a dish of toast soaked in warm milk, she nosed around the bag of pellet food which she loved, but Agnes thought she would not be able to manage it comfortably while her gums were still so torn and sore.

She shut Polly in the bedroom, locking the door behind her, and went down to the dining room. Whether it was the knowledge that Polly had been found and was now safe and recovering, or the fact that she had eaten practically nothing while she had been searching, Agnes suddenly felt hungry and she ordered the full breakfast: bacon, egg, a sausage and toast and marmalade. The girl brought half a grapefruit, too, with a smile.

'You need filling up, Mrs Turner – you've been starving yourself with worry. You must eat.'

Agnes enjoyed the meal but hurried a little eating it. She had to leave Polly for an hour this morning. She was reluctant to do so and, having returned to her room, waited till the maid had finished and, as usual, made a great fuss of Polly, and left. Agnes did not want the little dog disturbed while she was out. She was determined that what she had to do, the information she had to gain, was to be accomplished as quickly as possible. She settled Polly in her bed, told her – as she always did – that she wouldn't be long. Whether Polly understood her words or not, she curled up in her bed upside down, feet in air and tail wagging lazily.

Agnes checked her handbag, gave Polly a pat and locked the door behind her. She stood for a moment at the top of the stairs, her heart beating a little more quickly. She had things to do that she did not like, but they must be done. She went down the stairs; the receptionist smiled at her and came forward to the front of the big desk to ask after Polly, as she usually did almost whenever she met Agnes. Her concern was very genuine so Agnes always told her exactly how the little dog was progressing when she asked.

'She's better, thank you, and benefiting from all the kindness she has received here, believe me. I can never thank you all enough. I felt everyone was showing real concern.'

The receptionist was pleased and showed it.

'I'm going out but I hope to be back in an hour. The maid has done my room. I don't like leaving her but I'll be as quick as I can.'

Agnes left the manor and started up the familiar, and now detested, hill. She walked slowly, hoping she would not meet anyone coming up the hill behind her or coming down to go past – not a soul. Three-quarters of the way up Agnes knew she was at the spot, or very near, where Tracey hid the case. Looking round again, up and down the hill – no one. She pushed a little way through the undergrowth and there it was, the same case, in almost the same place – perhaps a little more securely hidden away. The lid opened easily, not even the two little latches at each end were properly closed. Agnes opened her handbag and took out the notes, two hundred pounds – an elastic band

148

holding the banknotes together. She put them in the case, under a sparkling sequin tank top. Then she opened her bag again and took out the little cardboard box containing the tablets, the little card of needles and the syringe. This she put in on top of the notes and pulled the top down to cover it, closing the case. This time she snapped the latches too; she wanted Tracey to know directly that she had deposited what she had asked in the case. She backed out of the tangled shrubs. The first thing she had come out this morning to do was done – now for the second thing. Agnes continued up the hill. This time she walked more hurriedly and with more resolution. At least she was not in possession of any drugs but Tracey was, and someone, Agnes was sure, would very soon find out that Tracey maybe was a dealer.

Next stop was the house and Thelma Ryman. Agnes had telephoned so she knew she was coming. She assumed a downcast expression. As far as Thelma was concerned, Polly was still missing, believed dead.

On Agnes's arrival, of course, Thelma asked the inevitable question: 'No sign of Polly?' even though an hour before she had asked the same question on the telephone. Agnes longed to give a sarcastic answer, like *'She hasn't appeared in the last hour, no Thelma,'* but she had no intention of offending her friend when she needed every bit of her co-operation. She just shook her head sadly and with eyes lowered, hiding the lie.

'I'm so sorry for you, Agnes, I really do believe I know how terrible you must be feeling, wondering. You loved her so much.'

Agnes nodded but made no attempt to tell Thelma the truth. Telling her the truth did not fit in with her plans at all. Thelma brought in the coffee which Agnes did not want after her substantial breakfast, but she sipped it for appearance's sake. The first lie came out almost with the first sip, Thelma this time.

'Well, at least Tracey hasn't got those drugs, Agnes. Whatever she was going to do with them she at least can't

149

take them now or get rid of them to other people, can she?'

Agnes took another sip of the unwanted coffee, and again shook her head.

'No, Thelma, at least she hasn't got the drugs now, which is some comfort I suppose.'

In spite of her optimism, Agnes sensed that Thelma was depressed – maybe because her daughter, her perfect daughter, had proved herself anything but perfect, but the next thing Thelma volunteered made Agnes think that her whole family were causing her to be depressed.

'I seem to spend my whole time alone, Agnes. Jerry has taken off back to London without even thanking me for all I have done for him, cooking, washing. I didn't take an interest in his painting, I admit.'

Agnes, nodding sympathetically, sipped more coffee.

'Richard, as I told you, spends all his time at the golf club. If the rain's pouring down he still goes. Sits in the club house and drinks with his friends. I haven't even met any of them, Agnes.'

She got out a tissue from her pocket and dabbed her eyes. Agnes felt Thelma was wallowing in self-pity.

'And Tracey, well, I simply don't understand her any more. She likes to be at Denise's house rather than here. Perhaps she finds me dull?'

'Is Tracey coming home this weekend, Thelma?'

'Yes, she's told her father to call for her tonight. He does exactly as she tells him, Agnes. Takes no notice of me at all.'

She stood up to get more coffee, which Agnes refused.

'He spoils her, I believe he would do anything for her, far more than he would for me. Perhaps he even knows what she's up to. I don't know, she's so secretive now.'

Agnes was not interested any more in the Ryman problems, but she just had to ask the question:

'Why don't you ask your husband why he spoils Tracey and does everything she tells him to do?'

Thelma looked at Agnes almost in astonishment.

'I have, Agnes, so many times. I've accused him of loving his daughter more than me, many times.'

Agnes got up; she was more than ready to leave, anxious to get back to her beloved Polly.

'What's his reply, his excuse for the way he behaves? And how does Tracey behave towards you?'

Thelma shrugged her shoulders and placed her hand over her eyes, her voice was muffled. 'She despises me, looks down on me, thinks I am weak and spineless, and really who can blame her? I do the washing, the ironing for them all, the cooking; they just expect me to cater for them. I'm a housekeeper, nothing more.'

Agnes picked up her handbag and made for the door. She had done the two things she had intended to do, got the information she wanted and dumped what she wanted to dump. She was not in the position to act or give advice to Thelma. Neither did she want to. She tried to make her goodbye as genial and friendly as it always had been. Thelma accompanied her to the gate as she usually did and gave her the usual quick kiss on the cheek.

'See you again soon, I hope, Agnes. Goodbye and I really pray you will have some news of Polly soon. Poor little pet.'

Agnes walked away from the house, looking back just once to see if Thelma had disappeared inside. Sometimes she would stand at the gate watching Agnes's progress down the hill and waving, if and when Agnes looked back with an answering wave. Proof, perhaps, that the woman was lonely and felt deserted and even used by her unresponsive family. Agnes at the moment, however, was not in a mood to sympathize. She paused at the place where Tracey's case was hidden and wondered as she did so what Thelma would do, how she would react, if she knew about the contents – the sequinned short top, the minuscule skirt, the high-heeled shoes and the fishnet tights. Agnes felt a smile creasing her lips – and what would Richard Ryman think of the contents? Disbelief probably, but he would be too frightened to face his daughter and forbid her wearing them. What a weak man he must be. No one in that little family could match Tracey for sheer strength of will to get whatever she wanted, come what may, and not care a jot who she hurt or undermined.

When she arrived back at the hotel after less than an hour away, Polly came out of her bed, favouring her foot from which the claw had been torn out. She greeted Agnes with almost all her usual enthusiasm, but she still looked painfully thin. Agnes had only just taken off her cardigan when there was a tap on her door. It was the waiter who had come with the warm milk yesterday when she had first brought Polly back. He was holding a little white dish which he carried into the room. Polly could smell what was in the dish. She limped around his feet, ready for the meal, but the waiter would not let her have it until he had checked it with her mistress.

'Bread and milk, just warm, Mrs Turner, and I've crumbled a digestive biscuit in the milk. OK?'

'Thank you so much, Leslie, you are so thoughtful. Polly has a lot of friends in this hotel, hasn't she?'

He put the small bowl on the floor by Polly, who set to at once, the soft biscuit adding a bit more taste to the bread and milk. The dish was licked clean in no time at all, much to the waiter's pleasure.

'There you are, mate, not much but you are not allowed beef and Yorkshire yet, old girl. But you soon will be, won't you?'

He picked up the dish and made for the door. Agnes knew better than to offer him a tip. He would, she knew from past experience, be most offended. But she was determined to do so, when she left the hotel at last, probably in the near future, if all went according to her plans.

After Leslie had gone, she carried Polly downstairs and along to Pooh Corner, brought her back and put her on the bed on her blanket. Polly stood up and would have jumped off the bed, she was so much better and more lively, but Agnes was determined to let her do very little until she had seen the vet again. She had already made the appointment to see him on Monday, maybe the day she would go home if she had done all she had to do.

Agnes decided not to go out and leave Polly again that day. She had lunch in the dining room and then went up to her room and lay on the bed beside Polly. She gave a lot of thought to Tracey's actions, what she would do after finding that the money and the drugs had been left in the case. Would she telephone Agnes or would she, Agnes, have to telephone the girl? And what would she say when she was asked to return Polly – would she go to the allotment and find the little dog had gone? What excuse would she come up with, what lie would she have to tell? The absence of the dog would be a blow to her, no reason to ask for more money. Or would she pretend the dog was still there, having been faithfully fed and watered? Whatever she said, Agnes would know it was just another untruth, just another blackmailing ploy. Tonight when her father brought her home, would she steal out to the case to check if the money and the pack of drugs had been placed there as she had demanded? Probably her mother would tell her that Agnes had called in this morning and was still very upset that little Polly had not been found. Agnes wondered how Tracey would react.

Agnes was to discover Tracey's reaction much sooner than she had anticipated. After dinner she came straight back upstairs to her room, gave Polly another small meal and settled down on the bed, Polly beside her, to continue reading her book. She had not been reading for more than ten minutes before her telephone rang. It was Tracey. Agnes waited for the girl to speak first.

'Well, Mrs Turner, how sensible of you. Hope you didn't keep any of the drugs yourself though?'

'No, I did not, Tracey, and I suggest you destroy them and don't do anyone any more harm with them than, in all probability, you have done already.'

There was a pause and Tracey giggled a little.

'When can I have Polly back? How is she, are you looking after her properly? Is she getting food and water?

It's almost a week you have had her now, Tracey, I want her back. I have done all you asked of me, but you can imagine how worried I am about my dog.'

Tracey answered rather more quickly this time. 'Oh, Polly's quite all right, Mrs Turner, I saw her today – gave her food and water. She's full of beans. Getting to quite like me, I think.'

Agnes could barely restrain her anger at the girl's lies. 'Full of beans' – how could she describe the dog's plight in that heartless way? Agnes bit back the words she longed to say: that Polly was here beside her.

'You say you saw her today, Tracey? Then why didn't you bring her back with you?'

'How could I explain that to my father, Mrs Turner? No, I'll get her later, but I've had a slight change of plan, another thought, if you know what I mean?'

Agnes tried to control her impatience and frustration.

'What do you mean – "another thought"?'

Then she listened while Tracey explained 'another thought'. She said her mother had told her that Agnes had been very upset about Polly not being found; indeed that she had nearly cried when she mentioned that her little dog was still missing. This, Tracey went on, had made her think 'another thought'. She had decided that if Mrs Turner was so upset about her dog, she would surely pay more than two hundred pounds to get her back – say another two hundred pounds?

Agnes could hardly believe what Tracey was suggesting. She had to switch off the telephone in order to give herself time to think, and not to give everything away by saying that she had Polly beside her and knew that Tracey was not telling the truth when she said she had seen the dog today. She called back; she knew the number well as Tracey was calling from the house on the hill.

'What happened, Mrs Turner, did you ring off?' Tracey had picked up the receiver at once so she had not left the telephone – the pause had worried her.

'I don't know how you can ask for more money, Tracey.

I certainly won't give you any more unless you bring Polly back, safe and sound, to me this evening. I can drive you there and back.'

Agnes wondered how she was going to get out of the problems that must beset her. No Polly to fetch. Tracey had her own ideas about getting round that.

'No, Ma and Daddy would wonder where I was going. You put the extra money in the case. I'm going out Saturday night,' and she gave that little giggle again. One could tell she was enjoying baiting her quarry. That Polly was not there seemed not to worry her at all.

Before Agnes could say any more the telephone went dead. She put down the receiver and leaned back against the headboard. She was pretty sure that Polly had been totally neglected while she had been shut up. The remark that Tracey had seen her today – did that mean she had actually been to the allotment and discovered that Polly was no longer there, had escaped, managed to force her way through that cruel latched door and got away? How would Tracey eventually deal with her absence? Never admit to it, Agnes guessed. Wait perhaps, continue with her demands until at last she had to say that Polly was dead. Was that how the malign young girl intended to end it?

Chapter Fifteen

Agnes did not sleep well that night; she was plagued by dreams about Tracey and Polly. Though she had her hand on the little dog as she lay on the bed beside her, she kept having dreams, or rather nightmares, as she relived breaking the latch on that box-like prison in the allotment, finding Polly, sitting there frightened and hurt, covered with excrement, blood round her mouth and blood splattered round the floor of the box. She kept dreaming Polly was still there, blaming herself for failing to find her in her searches. Agnes dozed off and woke again and again, sweating. In one of these horrible hallucinations she found herself sitting bolt upright, her legs already over the side of the bed, ready to go out and search for the animal who was on the bed beside her, looking at her, brown eyes fixed on her, awakened no doubt by Agnes's sudden movement, maybe feeling the fear and the anxiety that had come flooding back. Agnes tried to settle back, but she was almost afraid to let herself fall asleep again in case the horrible nightmare came back. Towards morning she began to sleep a little more deeply and the dreams went away, but Agnes longed for the morning. She was always aware that her mental state, particularly to do with animal cruelty of any kind, was highly sensitive, perhaps too sensitive, but all her life she had acted and felt the same. It was a sensitivity she could hardly contain.

After coping with Polly's needs when at last the morning came, Agnes went into the dining room. Almost all the couples were new 'weekend breakers' and apart from a formal 'Good morning' had nothing to say to Agnes or to each other. The waitress at Agnes's table suggested she have the full breakfast as she had yesterday, but Agnes refused with a smile. She felt that though the little waitress was about half Agnes's age, she had formed a bond with her, probably due to her long stay at the Manor Hotel. She was almost motherly and hoped to persuade Agnes to build up her strength.

'Toast and marmalade, coffee and orange juice,' Agnes said firmly and the girl complied and went off to get the order with only a shake of her head and a muttered, 'You should eat, you know, Mrs Turner.'

Polly was in much better spirits and no longer bleeding from her teeth and gums but the lost, pulled-out claw was still giving her a little trouble. Agnes decided to ring Amy with a progress report and to confirm her intention of returning home on Monday if all had gone according to plan. Amy was delighted.

'You seem to have been away such a long time, Agnes.'

Agnes answered with a certain amount of caution: 'Well, I may not make it on Monday, but I will ring you on Sunday evening, Amy, to let you know if I'm coming or not. I will know by then.'

As she put the receiver back on the rest it rang. This time it was Tracey telephoning.

'I'm home and I've checked the case, Mrs Turner. You don't seem to have understood. I want the extra two hundred pounds now. I expected it last night; it's not there this morning either. I've been and looked.'

Agnes's voice was firm. She looked over at Polly, who was trying to chew a Bonio. She felt she held the ace card.

'No, Tracey, you won't find the money there, not until you bring my dog back to me, safe and sound. The time is entirely up to you, not to me.'

'Well, you won't see Polly until I see the money, Mrs Turner. She is OK. I can keep her as long as I like. If you are as upset as Ma said you were, surely you won't miss a few hundred pounds?'

'I'm not sure, Tracey, how you are treating her. I want her back with me today, this morning.'

'Well, no money, no Polly, Mrs Turner.'

The receiver went down with a bang. Tracey must be furious that her prisoner had got away. How could she handle it? Well, Agnes thought, she had chosen the only way she could: refuse to produce the little dog because she no longer had her. Get the money and perhaps then tell some lie, or maybe the truth that the dog had got out, disappeared.

Agnes was debating how she could spend the morning, wondering if she would drive Polly up to the downs where the turf was smooth and springy, let her walk a little way, try the sore foot out a little. As she was trying to decide if there was a risk perhaps of the foot reinfecting, the telephone rang again. It was Jeremy Ryman. He sounded desperate.

'Jeremy, I heard from your mother yesterday that you had gone to London. Why are you back on the Island, what happened?'

'May I come and see you, Agnes, this morning?'

Agnes was reluctant to see the boy again. She felt she had had enough of the Ryman family, yet she liked Jeremy and so suggested meeting him in Newport for lunch. He agreed to this, but qualified her suggestion by a remark she didn't quite understand. What, she wondered, was the big favour?

'OK, Agnes, but I've got to ask a big favour of you, a very big favour. If you say no, well, I certainly won't blame you, be sure of that, Agnes.'

No mention of Polly. Maybe he didn't know she had been – and to all intents and purposes was still – lost. The situation was getting more and more muddled and intentions getting more and more obscure. Agnes arranged a time and place to meet – the Black Cat at twelve, midday. The Black Cat was a quiet little café in a back street of

Newport. Once more Polly would have to be left at the hotel. If Jeremy asked about Polly and wondered why she wasn't with Agnes, she would tell him that she had hurt her foot and was resting it up. Anyway, knowing the boy a little now, she thought he would be, by the sound of it, so preoccupied by the favour he was about to get from her, he would probably be quite unable to think of anything else but himself.

Agnes arrived at the Black Cat Café. It was almost empty, maybe because twelve o'clock was a little early for lunch. Jeremy was already seated at one of the Formica tables. He got to his feet the moment he saw Agnes enter the door and came forward to greet her. He looked white and drawn.

'Agnes, thank you so much for coming here to see me and listen to my tale of woe.'

He tried to smile as he spoke, but he made a very poor job of it. Agnes led the way towards the rear of the café, well away from the windows. Jeremy and she sat down at a table – Formica again, with a large plastic tomato and salt and pepper shakers standing rather forlornly in the middle. A white-aproned young waiter came up to them. Agnes looked towards Jeremy and asked him what he would like. He waved her question away and ordered coffee for both of them. The waiter nodded and made his way back to the counter, a hissing noise, and he returned with two cups of coffee, a little brown packet of sugar in each saucer. Jeremy took time to tear open the little packet and empty the sugar into his cup. Agnes felt he was playing for time and suddenly felt sorry for him.

'What is the trouble, Jeremy? How do you feel I can help you – is it about your painting career?'

Jeremy shook his head and did not look at Agnes. He kept his eyes down, focused on the cup of coffee. For a moment he was silent, then his problem all came rushing out, and ended: 'So I want you, if you will, Agnes, to lend me some money, say four hundred pounds, and I will pay you back, I absolutely promise you.'

159

That was the almost ashamed request, tagged on to a story which involved his sister, Tracey, as Agnes had already guessed. Wherever problems existed, it seemed she was at the heart of them, scheming, plotting, making the money to carry on her trade in drugs, or to buy anything she felt she wanted and was determined to get.

Jeremy and his father had managed to have a very friendly and constructive talk; really, they had never managed it before. The boy had been delighted when Richard had asked to see his paintings. He had seen one or two before and dismissed them almost without a glance. This time he had studied the whole portfolio carefully. Jeremy had sat beside him, watching his reactions to each of his creations, his beloved paintings into which, as he put it, he had poured out all the feelings and love for the subject he was setting down on the canvas in front of him.

'I didn't know, Jeremy. I didn't know what you could do. I've never bothered to find out, really, have I? I'm sorry, but with one thing and another – you know how it is.'

Jeremy said he had felt like crying, but he had not even let tears come to his eyes.

'Dad has no time for weakness, Agnes, he would not have understood it, hated it as emotional rubbish. So I kept a very stiff upper lip. Then he asked me would I like to go and live in London or would I rather live in France?'

Jeremy paused to take a sip of his cooling coffee. He was not so afraid of showing his emotions to Agnes and there were tears in his eyes as he put his cup down and continued:

'He gave me five hundred pounds, telling me he would support me and to come home when I wanted to. He was really like a father, Agnes, for the first time.'

'Well, that sounds wonderful, Jeremy. What kind of problem has that aroused? Why did you need to tell all this to me? It should have made you happy!'

'It did, Agnes, until my dear sister Tracey found out something about me and then demanded I give her the five hundred and make my way as best I could, or she would tell my father what she had found out. She knows Dad well and is very close to him for reasons I have already told you, haven't I, Agnes?'

'Yes, Jeremy, I know Tracey has got a pretty strong hold over your father, but that doesn't apply to anything she knows about you?'

'She found a letter from my partner, a love letter. I'm gay, Agnes, and if my father found out he would go spare, he is outraged by homosexuality. He won't even speak of it. If he knew his son was what he calls "a queer" he would never speak to me again. Further than that, he would never allow me in his house. He calls it unchristian, dirty, sinful. I have heard him ranting since I was about fourteen and was realizing then that I was . . . well, not like the other boys.'

Jeremy broke down and put his hand over his eyes. Agnes leant back in her chair and looked at him. She felt no compassion at all. What a weak, divided, stupid family, she thought; it made her feel glad she never had any family. She waited a moment or two before she spoke to him, gathering her thoughts together and not letting too many of her feelings show.

'Jeremy, I have seen – as you know – some of your paintings. I am not an art critic but I thought they were good. I enjoyed looking at them. As far as I can say, you have a real talent.'

Jeremy took his hand away from his face and his eyes met hers. They were grateful and yet questioning.

'So Tracey demanded the money. If you didn't give it to her she threatened to show your father the love letter. I presume I am right, Jeremy, so you let her have it? Silly, I think, I should have told her to tell your father if she wanted to and get on with it.'

He nodded miserably and did not answer her for a moment or two. Agnes had a fleeting thought that she might never see the money again, but what did it matter? She opened her handbag, took out her cheque book and made out a cheque for five hundred pounds. She slid it across the table towards him. At his promise to repay the amount, she shrugged her shoulders. She got up and touched the boy's hand in a gesture of farewell. She felt there was nothing else to say to him.

'Well, I suppose you felt you had to go along with her. If you had refused to give her the money, she could have ruined the relationship between you and your friend too. Pay me back one day and now, goodbye, Jeremy. Take care of yourself.'

She turned before he could answer and walked out of the café. Jeremy had sprung to his feet to accompany her to the door. She smiled at him.

'Thank you, Agnes, so very much,' he murmured as she walked away.

Agnes did not look back at him but she felt slightly sorry. 'Don't forget to pay for the coffee, will you?' she called back to him as she opened the café door. He shook his head and made his way to the counter. She just heard his last remark to her as the door swung to behind her and the traffic noise took over.

'The sale of my first picture I hope will be soon, Agnes, and that money I will send you. I promise I will repay you.'

I wonder, she thought rather than said as the traffic noise really took over. I wonder, then remembering the boy's eyes when they had been raised to hers at the table, the cooling coffee, the cheque, she got into her car and had another, more positive thought. *I believe him – they can't all be liars.* That thought amused her a little and she relaxed, started the car and began the drive back to someone who never lied or cheated and didn't even know how to be a blackmailer – Polly: how much she loved that little dog!

As she drove home, Agnes was haunted by a feeling of disbelief. During her life, she had known evil people, both men and women, but none of them she felt could compare with this girl Tracey Ryman. Not yet fifteen years old, little more than a child, yet she seemed to have no love or even fondness for anyone in her family. Perhaps there were

162

others she felt something for. Agnes remembered the quick embrace she had seen in the road below the hill, just before the two had boarded the bus. Had that been her first sight of Tracey? Yes, she thought, it was. So much had happened between the girl and herself since that brief glimpse. Agnes also remembered she had rather admired the girl's daring, thought she was perhaps feeling hemmed in, trapped by a rather fussy old-fashioned family. When she had learned more about the girl, that trace of admiration had turned to disgust and loathing: the girl's behaviour to her father, to her brother, the nuns at the London convent, and now to Polly and herself. Agnes wondered, would Denise last as a friend? Would she commit some act that would put her on to Tracey Ryman's blackmailing list? Tracey's mother seemed to be the only person who still adored her and could find no fault in the girl. Probably the poor woman had never done anything to merit blackmail. What a situation!

Before she left Newport, Agnes had searched out and found the vet's surgery. She wanted to buy Polly another boot for her sore foot and try and persuade her that it was not just a toy. The girl in the vet's outer office showed Agnes several sizes. One looked about Polly's size of paw and Agnes bought it without much hope that her little dog would let her put it on, let alone wear it.

'Is that for the little dog who was shut away – Mrs Turner, isn't it?'

Agnes was a little surprised that the young woman knew about Polly's adventures and horrors, sounding interested and sorry about it all.

'Mr Campbell told me about her, furious he was, he said if he had his way he would shut up the people who did it in a similar condition and leave them without food or water for a week or so. He would too!'

Agnes smiled, paid for the little boot and thanked the girl. It was nice to know that Mr Campbell felt so strongly about Polly.

Polly greeted her with delight when she returned. Agnes

carried her down the stairs but she walked through the hall and back garden to Pooh Corner. She was quite agile on three legs, with an occasional use of the fourth, very tentatively. Back in her room Agnes tried on the little bootee. It was made of leather with a lining of nylon or sheepskin. Polly permitted it to be tried on, but a minute later she had got it off and was tossing it up in the air. It flew under the dressing table and Polly spread-eagled, nosing into the very small space underneath. She was blowing into the crack and growling with frustration. Agnes felt relieved to see her so playful. She felt herself smiling broadly, almost laughing – the first time she had done so since her pet's disappearance. She wondered how she had managed to get through that awful time of anxiety and distress without relapsing into her black depression.

At that moment the telephone rang. To Agnes's surprise, it was Jeremy thanking her again for lending him the money. He insisted once more that he intended to pay her back when he sold his first picture. He said one thing about which Agnes had to agree with him.

'You seem to have seen and heard the worst of my family, except Ma. Tracey – well, I can't understand how she can go to these awful lengths, Mrs Turner. I should have guessed, I suppose, after the nuns and Dad, but I didn't know she would ever turn on me like this.'

Agnes could only try to reassure him, but there was so much more he didn't even guess about his sister. All he knew were the few things Tracey had to boast about to build up her own ego. He was taking off straight away – he had his passport with him. He said he never wanted to see his sister again, and would go straight to France after collecting his things in London. He finished off by repeating again his promise regarding the loan.

'I hope you realize I mean it, Mrs Turner – Agnes?'

'I know you do, Jeremy, and I expect to hear from you, not about the money, though I know you mean that too, but mostly of your success as a painter, you know that.

164

I really mean it, too. I shall be so interested to hear from you, how you are getting on, so write to me.'

Agnes placed the receiver back in its cradle. She liked the boy, weak perhaps, too reliant on his parents, but so many young people were. She wondered if he had said goodbye to his mother. She tried for the moment to dismiss all thoughts of the Rymans from her mind and help Polly retrieve her little boot. She couldn't feel it by thrusting her fingers as far as she could. The dressing table was a solid, old-fashioned piece of furniture, much too heavy for her to move. With the same little smile on her face that Polly had caused, Agnes pulled out the drawer and took out the object she had hidden there, wrapped in her headscarf. She took off the scarf and there it was in her hand, the much sought-after kitchen knife. She dropped down on her knees. She thrust the blade of the knife under the dressing table and swished it to and fro. The little boot flew out across the floor, much to Polly's excitement and delight. She grabbed the boot and threw it up in the air. It landed on the bed, too high for Polly to jump up. Agnes picked her up and put her on the bed, where she settled down to have a good chew.

Agnes got to her feet, still holding the knife, and wrapped it carefully back in the scarf. This time, however, she did not return it to the drawer. She laid it almost gently on the top of the table beside her make-up and jars of cream – all her things in daily use. She shut the drawer and for some time she stood looking at the covered knife – put a hand out and stroked the silk of the headscarf. Then she turned away to play with Polly, still smiling. She had eaten little today since breakfast. She decided she would shower, change into a dark dress – the navy one – and go down to the dining room and try to eat a good dinner. She felt hungry already but she would wait till dinner, then enjoy her meal all the more.

She stretched out on the bed beside Polly, who was asleep, feet in the air, a gesture of doggy contentment and relaxation. Agnes noticed that the game with the leather boot had made the little dog's gums bleed again. Luckily the hotel was still delivering soft foods for her. Agnes took the boot away. She would have to find a very soft woolly toy – the leather boot was too hard. How weird it was, she thought as she lay there, the amount of grief a family could generate amongst themselves. Sometimes in her life she had felt depressed that she had no one, never even knew who her mother was, or her father, so no brothers or sisters, cousins, aunts, uncles. But the Rymans: just one bad apple amongst them and the misery it caused! What would happen if Tracey, as she grew up, became more criminally clever, what would she turn into? A black-mailer? Yes, she was that already. Drug dealer in a big, big way by the time she was twenty-five, thirty. What then? It was frightening even to think about it. What cruelties could she get up to, to animals and humans – particularly animals. She was evil, evil and without any kind of remorse.

Chapter Sixteen

Agnes came out of her room and closed the door sound-
lessly behind her. She looked at her watch – twenty past
midnight. Agnes had taken a gamble on the night porter
being away from the large reception counter in the hall: the
gamble had come off. Two or three times when she had
come in late, the porter had been in the kitchen having his
dinner, or at least preparing it. Tonight, as she came down
the stairs, she saw the chair behind the reception counter
was empty and the light in the kitchen was shining
through the two porthole-like circles of glass in the doors.
Some time ago he had told Agnes with some pride that he
had learned how to use the microwave and it was now
easy to make himself a hot meal, or to heat a bedtime drink
for any of the residents who came in late and wanted
one.

Agnes turned at the bottom of the stairs and walked
silently through the sitting room. The hall was almost in
darkness, the sitting room slightly lighter. The french
windows at the end of the room were not locked and she
was able to slide one back and let herself out into the
back garden of the manor. So far, so good. She reached
Pooh Corner, stepped over the fallen planks – thoughts of
Polly and her dreadful week went through her mind as she
did so. Through the rather rough field to the main road,
deserted at this time of night – only one car went by as she
walked the short way to the leafy, muddy, hardly discern-
ible path down which the murdered man had slid on that
fatal night when he had met his death. Agnes consulted

her watch once more – twenty-five to one. It was dark but the glimmer from a street lamp some way away illuminated the dial just enough for her to read it.

As she approached the little side path she was aware of her heart beating again a little faster than usual. She started the ascent which she knew would take her up to just opposite the place where the briefcase was hidden, or had been hidden and, according to Tracey, was still hidden.

Something on the ground beside her foot made Agnes recoil. It looked like a snake, a small one perhaps, but Agnes had a horror of snakes – about the only animal she was afraid of, but even a snake she would not harm. She peered a little closer, moving her foot, then she could see what had so unnerved her. It was a short length of the yellow and blue tape the police had used to mark off the area surrounding the body; a piece cut off and thrown away, half covered with mud and debris. Agnes breathed a sigh of relief and continued on, crushing as she walked the soft rotting leaves, not using what little path there was. The smell of rotting leaf mould and mud and rainwater reminded her again of Polly and how she loved digging and tearing about after imaginary animals.

She continued on to the top of the hill where the path merged with the wider one she was used to. Still very little light now, but more than there had been coming up the small incline. There was a moon, but it was almost obliterated by slow-moving black clouds. Now and again the horizon – seemingly far away – was lit for seconds by a flash of sheet lightning. Agnes hoped that if a storm was to come it would at least hold off till Tracey had made her way up the hill, found the case, changed her clothes and left her disguise behind. Which, Agnes wondered, was the disguise? The tracksuit or the fishnet tights, tiny skirt, revealing top, showing already well-formed breasts; the incredible shoes that made the girl two inches taller? All expensive items, particularly the shoes. No wonder the girl needed more money for clothes she could never take to her room. Where would she hide them? Agnes could imagine Thelma saying, 'Tidy your room, Tracey, put your things away, do you want anything washed?' Tracey would, she was sure, boil with rage and call it 'an invasion of privacy' which, in a way, it was. Then Ma, as Tracey called her, would probably start to look in the drawers and wardrobe herself. Mothers of fourteen-year-old girls do. The risk must be too great for the girl to take it, hence the hidden case.

If Agnes was right, all would work out as she wished and had imagined. She remembered Tracey's giggle as she had spoken about Polly – '*I'm going out Saturday night.*' Well, Agnes thought, now was the testing time. She drew behind a large bush in an area of thick undergrowth, nettles, ferns, blackberries. The brambles pulled at the trousers of her black jogging suit. She had put on a pair of disposable gloves she used to tidy up after Polly had done her business. Fingerprints would not be made through the material, but her hands felt hot and sticky. Her heart rhythm had slowed down to normal. This was more comfortable. She waited – eyes fixed on the path below her, waiting, waiting. She knew the moped, if it arrived, would alert her when it drew up at the foot of the pathway on the main road. Perhaps it would not come, perhaps Tracey had changed the date, or maybe the moped had broken down, or the boy Douglas had opted out? Perhaps anything. Agnes could only wait. She was good at waiting, patient and still. She leant, stiff-backed, against the tree behind her, the knife blade cold against her thigh. The handle of the knife was held safely against her waist by the elastic waistband of her trousers, ready to pull out quickly and silently when it was needed. She felt a thrill of pleasure at her own neat arrangements. She had thought of everything. Premeditation was new to Agnes – usually she acted as the moment dictated, using whatever was to hand. This was not perhaps quite to her liking, but then – as the saying has it – circumstances alter cases. Something moved near her foot. It was too dark to see what it was: something small, scurrying about its innocent business – perhaps a field mouse or a shrew. Agnes registered the occurrence in her mind – she must not step on the little creature when she left, must not frighten it to death by a clumsy, heavy movement. She would remember: she didn't want to hurt it.

Her thoughts were suddenly interrupted, not by a mouse as she had half expected, but by a light. The moped drew up at the foot of the path, almost noiselessly. The moon obliged Agnes for just a minute. She saw a girl get off the back of the bike – she did so carefully. Agnes guessed Tracey would be careful of her tights, careful of the short, tight skirt, the hideous – but to Tracey, trendy – and probably expensive shoes. Agnes could see very little. The sky seemed to be growing darker. At that moment, as if to help her, the bus came round the corner, its lights illuminating the scene for a few seconds. Tracey was just handing her helmet to the boy. The bus did not stop and the scene blacked out again. Did the boy remove his helmet, did the pair embrace, kiss goodnight? Agnes guessed they did because a few seconds passed, then the moped's light moved and the engine roared a little. 'See you, Doug!' – her voice almost yelled the words and Agnes stiffened as the girl's scramble up the hill began. In those shoes, on that surface, Agnes guessed it was, indeed, a scramble. She heard the girl's 'Damn!' as she slipped. When Tracey got further up the hill and was drawing almost opposite Agnes, another gift of light happened – a car down below on the road lit the scrambling figure and shone on the blue glittery top she was wearing. Her face showed white, her eyes fixed on the ground, choosing her steps. She passed Agnes, who could hear now every rather laboured breath taken. She touched the wooden handle of the knife at her waist. The wood felt strange through the plastic glove. She loosened her grip, then, her rubber-soled shoes making no sound, she followed the girl, her hand impatient. But she was careful, the moment must be right. *Not yet, not yet,* she whispered to herself: *wait, wait, wait.*

Tracey reached the top of the little hill and Agnes paused, too. The girl did not move for at least half a minute. She staggered again: this time she put up her hand and held the side of her head for a moment as if she had a headache, then she straightened up and went on. She started to cross the lane-like part of the hill towards the case. This took her a little higher up and to the right, for the moment excluding her from Agnes's vision. Agnes hurried a little and a twig snapped under her foot. Tracey turned round and looked down the way she had come. Agnes had drawn back, but the girl seemed reassured and started to push her way through the gap she had made in the dense tangle of growth. Agnes waited to hear the snap of the two catches as Tracey pressed them. Though she must have reached the case, there was no sound. Agnes waited seconds longer. She wanted to catch the girl at the right moment, in her gear, not changed into her climbing clothes. Agnes felt there was no need for more caution – she came forward across to where the girl was. Then another noise stopped her, a sound of retching, hard and prolonged. Tracey was vomiting on to the grass. Drink? Agnes wondered.

The sheet lightning was closer and one or two flashes, almost on top of each other, lit up the scene in front of Agnes like a black and white photograph. Tracey, facing her, looked already like death – her face ashen, her lips black. A stream of blood, again looking black in the storm light, flowed from her nostrils. She put up a hand to wipe it away, gazed at it, puzzled. She looked up and seemed only then to become aware of who was standing in front of her, knife in hand. She spoke, using the same words she had used last time they stood on this hill, not knowing that they were to be the very last words she would ever utter, her voice made guttural by the blood coming from her mouth:

'Mrs Turner, whatever are you doing here?'

Then Tracey fell forward. Her legs did not buckle, nor did she put out either hand to save herself. She just fell, flat, arms at her sides, bent at the elbows, hands open and relaxed, legs straight, slightly apart. Agnes noted a tear in one fishnet-covered leg – only the nylon torn, not the skin beneath. One shoe was half on, half off. No movement, no twitching, no sound. Agnes stood beside her, watching, then she at last bent down. She felt the wrist, searching for a pulse, found nothing, put her fingers on the carotid artery – disliking touching the girl. One look at the face, turned towards her, confirmed her knowledge that the girl was dead. She felt no sorrow, no compassion. Several people would feel relief and thankfulness that her power was gone. The blood from the nose was only oozing now, not pumping out as it had been. There was no pump going to force the blood out in spurts. Agnes got up, picked up the knife which she had dropped beside the dead girl as she examined her, and thrust it back against her thigh. One last look at the still figure and she turned away and began the walk down the hill to the manor, her only anxiety now to get back into the hotel without being seen or heard. As she walked, the thunder began to rumble; the storm was getting closer, the lightning brighter and more frequent. Agnes was glad she was on her way back. Polly was not too keen on thunder, not exactly scared but made uneasy and she had had enough stress lately. As to Tracey, Agnes wondered who would find the body. Richard Ryman would feel a sense of relief mixed with his sorrow, as would Jeremy, not to speak of Agnes herself.

Maybe others in the girl's drug-ridden world would be thankful too – a blackmailing mouth shut up for ever. Only Thelma would grieve. Her mother who, as far as Agnes knew, had never done anything which could cause her daughter to blackmail her, and was now worried about the drugs found on Tracey but would probably never believe that her dear innocent daughter took drugs herself. In the end, Thelma would be certain to convince herself that Tracey had become involved in the drug world by sheer accident. Another saying came to Agnes as she turned the corner into the rough field behind Pooh Corner: When

172

ignorance is bliss, it is folly to be wise. How very true that was in poor Thelma Ryman's case. Well, now she would never learn about her husband's infidelity, nor Richard the truth about his son's lifestyle.

Agnes crossed the field as quickly as she could. The temper of the storm was altering: raindrops, big and heavy, were splashing down as she walked. The lightning was now more forked than sheet. She stepped easily on the fallen planks that bordered the little half-shed, half-kennel that Polly always favoured. The thunder became more menacing and Agnes's heart rate went up again as she approached the garden path which ran up to the sliding windows of the hotel sitting room. Not a soul about, but a dim table light was on in the sitting room which made Agnes pause and conceal herself behind the curtains that bordered each side of the french windows. She ventured a little further – thank goodness the night porter had not yet got around to sliding the doors shut. Agnes stepped inside. She glanced at her watch – ten past two – went into the hall, round the bend of the stairs. She heard suddenly a noise from the small television room off the sitting room, a switching noise. It was the night porter switching off the television at the socket – pulling out the plugs for safety's sake, as he had no doubt been instructed to do, in a storm. It gave Agnes time to run up the stairs, unlock her door and close it silently behind her.

She leaned for a moment on the closed door, just for a moment, to get her breath back. She greeted Polly, who was sleepy but wagging her tail. She sat down on the side of the bed and as she did so she heard the night porter go by her door and into the next-door room which she knew was empty. He crossed the room – she heard him close the window. Outside the rain was beginning to pour down heavily, the storm becoming even more dramatic. Polly looked around, a little disturbed. Agnes picked her up and put her on the bed and lay down beside her. As she did so, she felt the knife against her thigh. She got up, wrapped it in the headscarf and put it on the dressing table. Back on

173

the bed, she began to think calmly over the night's happenings. Was she glad she had not had to use the knife? She wasn't sure. There would have been satisfaction there, but it might have been a messy business. As it was, it was cleaner, but had Tracey got her just end? Again, Agnes was not sure. That the girl was better dead she had no qualms about, but she had to admit she would have liked to be there when someone found the body. Maybe tomorrow morning.

Chapter Seventeen

Thelma wakened suddenly and lay for a moment wondering what had roused her. She looked across the bedroom, dimly lit by a small socket light Richard had insisted on having – he sometimes had to get up in the night and go to the bathroom. The upstairs hallway had a similar socket light. He didn't have to switch on the bedside light and wake Thelma. Richard could be thoughtful in some ways and thoughtless in others. In the light the socket afforded she could see that whatever had wakened her had certainly not disturbed him. They had twin beds and Thelma was able to see he had not stirred and his rhythmic snoring was as usual. Then Thelma realized it was the patter of rain on the window that probably had disturbed her. She thought of Tracey, or rather Tracey's window always open to its fullest extent. She would never close it even if it was raining heavily. The pattering raindrops seemed to be lessening. Thelma was warm and comfortable. Should she leave it and hope the rain would stop? She turned on her side and cuddled down under the duvet. Before she closed her eyes a quick flash of lightning lit the room and almost at once there came a crash of thunder. Thelma threw back the clothes and thrust her feet halfway into her slippers. She had better go and close her daughter's window or the carpet would get a soaking if the rain came back in storm force. She paused to pull up the backs of her slippers, glanced back at Richard as she left the bedroom, crossed the hall and opened Tracey's door, quietly so as not to waken her daughter.

The curtains billowed out as she entered the room and lightning flashed, illuminating the room. No Tracey. The bed was slightly disturbed, the duvet thrown back; the little bedside clock gleamed red telling the time to be twenty to three. Thelma pulled the window shut and drew the curtains. Where was Tracey? That she was in the house Thelma did not for one moment doubt. Perhaps she had an upset tummy or the storm had frightened her. Usually she was completely unmoved by thunder and lightning. Thelma crossed the landing – the bathroom door was shut. She opened it. No Tracey. Another thought – sometimes Tracey had crept downstairs to see a late night film with one of her favourite stars in it. Richard, usually so compliant towards his daughter, had made a rule that she was only to do such a thing if there was no school the next day. Tracey had obeyed the rule and the habit had died a natural death, but perhaps she was downstairs now, watching an old film with one of her 'great loves' in it. Or another idea – she might be in the kitchen making herself a hot drink, having been wakened, like her mother, by the storm. No television; the sitting room was in complete darkness. Thelma made for the kitchen. She rather wished Tracey was in there heating some milk for a drink. This had happened once or twice in London, when Tracey was about twelve. They had sat together at the kitchen table, drinking Ovaltine or cocoa – whatever was the most liked hot drink of the moment; Bovril or Oxo, even tea – never coffee. Thelma was certain at the time that coffee was bad for the young. She had never been closer to her daughter than at those 'midnight drinks' as they used to call them. Thelma had felt almost shy with Tracey when they talked together on these rare and rather precious occasions. Tracey had seemed so grown up, so wise, so sure of her own opinions, not arrogant but almost as if she was the one with more experience than the woman sitting opposite her, her mother. On those rare occasions Tracey had kissed her goodnight, something she never usually did. However, Thelma's hopes were dashed: the kitchen was in the same deserted darkness as the rest of the downstairs of the house. Thelma suddenly flew upstairs – had Tracey fainted and fallen down by her bed? She switched on the main light, but no girl lay on the floor on the other side of the bed.

The lightning flashed more frequently now and the thunder rumbled angrily round the skies. Tracey had gone to bed early, about nine o'clock, saying she was tired and wanted to read for a bit, then sleep. Denise's house is noisy, she had told them: 'It's nice and quiet here, I can have a good kip.' Yes, Thelma remembered her saying all that. It had pleased Richard. Usually Tracey was rather scathing about this house and said it was too like her grandmother – old-fashioned. Yes, she had said all that before going to bed, but where was Tracey now? When Thelma returned to their room, Richard had turned over and was facing the other way, but he hadn't wakened and his snore was just the same. She went across to his bed and shook his shoulder to waken him.

'Richard, Richard!' She had to shout, he was so fast asleep. He opened his eyes and then closed them again. Thelma almost hit him – Richard always took ages to wake up. Now he rubbed his eyes and gave a huge yawn.

'Richard, I can't find Tracey, she's not in the house. I've looked everywhere. Where can she be?'

Richard roused himself, got out of bed, grabbed his robe and shrugged into it. He shuffled around and, rather like Thelma had, thrust his feet into slippers and prepared to walk with them half on and half off. His slowness and complete lack of anxiety about Tracey infuriated her.

'Where can she be at this time, it's nearly three?'

'Tried the kitchen? Is she making herself a hot drink? This storm probably frightened her a bit.'

As if to confirm his words, the lightning flashed and the thunder rumbled almost at once. Richard gave himself to another huge yawn.

'Pretty close. I think I know what she's done.'

Richard walked back towards his bed and to Thelma's astonishment he took off his robe.

'When I picked her up, Denise was trying – and she was trying very hard – to get Tracey to stay and go with her to some party. Garage party, I think she called it. Anyway, Tracey wouldn't go, wanted to come home with me. Said she'd made other arrangements. Don't know why, she doesn't usually like missing a party, does she?'

He got into bed and pulled the duvet up around him.

'Look, Denise's boyfriend has been over here and fetched her with Denise. I expect she telephoned Tracey and persuaded her to go to this party. Could do with a cup of tea, old girl.'

Thelma was furious at Richard's easy explanation – stupid, in her opinion.

'Why didn't she let us know, telephone us? She uses that wretched mobile enough. Why didn't she phone us?'

The storm showed no sign of going away, indeed the rain was now torrential. Thelma was worried and not at all comforted by Richard's theories.

'I'll go and make us a cup of tea then, Richard.'

She made her way downstairs to the kitchen and filled and switched on the kettle. She wandered around the kitchen, trying to get herself to accept Richard's explanation. She admitted he knew how Tracey's mind worked a great deal better than she did. He was probably right. She made tea and took it upstairs. Richard looked comfortable; he had pulled one of his pillows up and was sitting up slightly in order to drink his tea. Thelma couldn't feel quite as relaxed. She sat on the side of her bed, still with her gown and slippers on, drinking her tea without much enjoyment.

'You worry too much, old girl, really you do. Teenagers go their own way these days, you can't stop them.'

'She's only fourteen, Richard, still a child. I know she acts grown up but she isn't.'

Thelma finished her tea and took Richard's cup from him.

He snuggled down, pulling the duvet up around his shoulders, shutting his eyes firmly. His wife carried the tea tray down to the kitchen and set the china on the draining board. She still felt disturbed, anxious. Where was Tracey? What was a garage party? Would she come back here or stay with Denise for the night? The storm was dying away a little. Thelma walked through the hall towards the stairs. She felt breathless; the storm was making the air humid. She went to the front door and opened it wide. A delicious draught of cooler air enveloped her, a small, less humid breeze. She drew it thankfully into her lungs. The thunder rumbled further off, but a sudden streak of lightning lit up the lane, hovered, showing up the grey trees, the tumbling water running down the hill. Then Thelma saw it, a body lying face down, the legs spread-eagled in the wet mud, the arms flung out each side. Thelma let out a shrill, piercing scream, went to the foot of the stairs and screamed again for Richard. He appeared at the top of the stairs, eyes wide.

'What the hell's the matter now, Thelma, what is it?'

But she had gone, down the path to the gate, and was wrenching it open. She was sobbing. The rain had stopped, but flashes still lit up the scene. Then Richard saw what his wife had seen.

'Oh, God, who is it, what is it, it's not . . .?'

'No, no, it's a girl, not Tracey, she doesn't dress like this. Poor girl, she's bleeding, look – from her back or her side or somewhere. She's dead, Richard, she's dead!'

'Looks like a prostitute, look at her legs and clothes.'

Richard turned the girl a little on her side, pushed back the soaking hair which looked black in the light of the flashes. But he recognized the dead face, blood still oozing from the mouth and nose. It wasn't a prostitute, it was his daughter.

'It's Tracey, Thelma, and she's been injured, punched – she's bleeding from her mouth, her nose! She's dead!'

Thelma, too, fell on her knees in the wet mud of the hill.

She tried to turn the body further over on its side to get a better look at the face.

'It's not Tracey, Richard, don't be silly. Look at the clothes, Tracey has no clothes like that. She would never dress like that, never.' Her voice had risen to a scream, disbelieving.

'I'll go and ring the doctor and the police. It is Tracey, Thelma, no matter how she is dressed.'

Thelma caught hold of his arm to stop him. 'Don't leave her out here alone. Let's get her into the house, into her bed. It's so awful out here.'

'She doesn't need her bed any more, Thelma.'

He stood up and paused for a moment, looking at the girl stretched out at his feet. Thelma looked up at him; he was quite dry-eyed, calm. He turned and made his way into the house. Thelma stayed on her knees beside the body. She gazed into her dead daughter's eyes. She still couldn't believe what she was seeing – yes, the face was Tracey's. She half rose to her feet, then sank down again. The legs, in those black net tights, a hole in one of them, torn. The minuscule red plastic-looking skirt – Tracey would never, never, never . . . the blue sparkly top hitched up to just under her breasts . . . Thelma began to lose control and started to scream, loud and long. Then her tears broke off her screaming.

'No, no, no, no, not Tracey. Not Tracey!'

Richard rang off and ran down the path out of the gate and joined his wife, trying to stop her screaming. He put his hands under her arms to lift her to her feet. It was no use – he could not move her. He was thankful when at last he heard the grinding noise of wheels coming up the hill. Either a police car or an ambulance – he couldn't tell, the ascending headlights blinded him. But ambulance or police car, it hardly mattered which – Tracey was beyond the help of either. He let go of his wife, let her sink down again and waited for whatever vehicle was coming up the hill.

'Come inside, Thelma, we can't do anything for her;

180

come inside until the police have finished and she's in the ambulance. Then they will let us . . .'

Thelma looked at him, her face expressionless, and eventually allowed him to lead her back to the house. In the sitting room she sat down abruptly on the settee.

'There was a butterfly, a butterfly on her shoulder at the back – orangey colour – pretty it was, a tattoo – I never knew it was there.' She put her hands up and covered her face. 'There must have been so much I didn't know about her.'

Richard looked at her, his face – like hers – almost expressionless. He sat down beside her, put his arm round her shoulders.

'You could say that, dear, so much we didn't know, but that's teenagers, isn't it? They are like that. Keep things to themselves.'

'Excuse me, sir, could you come outside – just you, I want a word.'

The uniformed policeman had a yellow waterproof over his uniform. He reached up to take his cap off. Then as Richard got up and began to follow him outside, the man seemed to change his mind and left it on. A WPC edged past him. She looked at Richard, then spoke to the policeman. She looked neat, healthy, fair hair swept back under the becoming hat. She said, 'I'll just see if I can do anything for Mrs Ryman.' Richard walked out of the front door, down the garden path, out into the still drizzling rain and the dying storm. He felt sick, numb, as if this were all happening in a film or on television.

The police were stretching the familiar yellow and blue tapes round the area – just as they had done with the other, Richard thought. But this time it was different. He thought of his wife's preoccupation with the butterfly. Tracey had had that done, probably while in Newport with Denise – leading a double life at fourteen. He thought of the tights with a curious, sexual thrill – who was she wearing them for? The tiny skirt – what else? The policeman appeared to understand his silence. There was a man there taking photographs, she would have liked that, Tracey – any form of attention! A plain-clothes policeman introduced himself. The flashlight from the camera rivalled the now diminished lightning. The detective put his hand on Richard's arm.

'I'm sorry, sir, we just want to confirm it is your daughter, sir – before we move her.'

Richard nodded, still dry-eyed. He felt shame at what he was feeling – relief. He turned to the man.

'Oh, yes, it is my daughter.' Then he broke down, covered his eyes with the handkerchief he had pulled from the pocket of his robe. He felt the tears forcing themselves from his eyes. He drew away from the body. They seemed now to be preparing to lift it on to the red blanket-covered stretcher. Then he noticed the black bag. Two policemen approached the body with the long plastic container – Richard didn't want to see that done. He wondered was he behaving as a man should behave? Then suddenly, he felt it really didn't matter much, she was dead. Tracey was dead, never to speak again. Silent for ever.

'Can I go back to my wife now?' he asked, his voice sounding thick, his throat hurting when he spoke. His chest hurt, too. Was he going to have a heart attack, a coronary?

The policeman nodded, took his arm again and propelled him forward, back to the house. The light made him blink. He could hardly see and bumped into a chair, found his way over to the sideboard and poured himself a stiff whisky. He did not offer one to Thelma.

Chapter Eighteen

Agnes, once safely back in her own room, had a weird feeling of unreality, as if there was no relation between what she had witnessed on the hill, and the quiet, darkened room in which she now found herself. She did nothing about the darkness, did not put a light on in case it roused Polly enough to make her want to go out. As it was, the little dog lay on her back in her bed, legs in the air and tail wagging lazily as she took in the fact that Agnes was back. She cuddled down in her bed, obviously realizing it was the middle of the night.

Agnes moved about the dark room, aided now and again by a flash of lightning. She took off her black jogging suit and threw it over the back of a chair. In her nightdress she went over to the dressing table and managed to pick out her large jar of cleansing cream from among the array of bottles and tubes. She sat down at the dressing-table mirror and cleaned her face, trying to pick out her features in the dim darkness. Now and again a flash illuminated her face. She looked pale, or so she thought, but maybe it was the grey scene the lightning appeared to make of the grass and trees outside her windows. In the bathroom she was just as quiet. Then she climbed into bed, feeling she would not sleep. She piled up the pillows behind her and reached for her book. She would read, then try and forget the hillside scene.

The rain still pattered on the window; it seemed to be increasing rather than decreasing. She looked at the little clock by her bed. It was almost an anticlimax, the girl's death, the blood, the quick collapse. Agnes had read quite a lot about the side effects of drugs – morphine, heroin, crack, acid. Ecstasy was rather more of an unknown quantity, some of the tablets being made by unscrupulous people who, as long as it would turn into a recognizable tablet, would put in any drug they could get hold of. Some perhaps could cause bleeding, collapse and death. Obviously the bleeding had been happening elsewhere in the girl's body, causing her instantaneous death. Agnes remembered the girl staggering a little as she reached the top of the hill, and before. She had put it down to alcohol, thinking the girl was drunk. Maybe she had been wrong. Maybe the girl had been close to death then. Agnes remembered the girl's words, a replay from that earlier death – *'Mrs Turner, whatever are you doing here?'* Agnes had had no time to answer the question before the girl had hit the ground. Not another sound had come from her, not even a breath. A strange death. Agnes could just see the knife on the dressing table, sheathed with the headscarf. She was glad she had not had to use it. The girl's death had solved her difficult problem. She felt a mild curiosity about the cause of death. Ten to four. She could not go home until Monday. It would look odd if she left at once – did not talk to the grieving mother. Also she must tell Thelma that Polly had been found. There would be no mention of anything that the blackmailer had done.

She put aside her book – reading was out of the question – and glanced again at the green numbers on her bedside clock: ten past four. She flattened her pillows, and as she did so she heard the wail of a police car or maybe an ambulance. They had found the body much sooner than Agnes had expected. Who had found the girl? A courting couple – surely not in this weather? Anyway it was nothing whatever to do with her. Agnes felt ready for sleep now. The ambulance would clear up the mess; take the body to the morgue. It was nothing whatever to do with her. She closed her eyes, trying to shut out the scene and noises.

Agnes did not sleep well, indeed what was left of the night was horrible. Dreams and nightmares disturbed her: sometimes she half woke but the dream carried on. Blood figured in each dream: muddled, the red flow sometimes coming from Polly, then Tracey. Then the girl was grinning at her, holding the little dog in her arms, and taking no notice of the blood flowing from her nose. Agnes woke at about six o'clock. The storm had died away, but Agnes did not sleep again. She kept herself determinedly awake rather than face the dreams again. She was not usually so affected. As a nurse she had faced death and patients drifting into comas without any emotion. Maybe if she had done as she had intended, plunged in the knife, paid back the pain and fear Polly had been put through, maybe then she would not have been so conscious of the drama of the girl's sudden death. She felt cheated of her revenge. Agnes understood her own feelings. She picked up the knife, still on the dressing table, took off the headscarf and looked at the blade shining in the morning light. It seemed to have a beauty of its own. Agnes wrapped it up again, opened the drawer and pushed the weapon to the back, well out of sight but not entirely out of her mind. She must dispose of it one day, but at the moment it could lie there in the dark, its silvery sparkle not sullied again – used once but that was it.

Breakfast time – Agnes put on Polly's lead to take her for the accustomed walk through the garden. The grass smelled fresh and lovely, the flowers beginning to stand up again after the drenching the storm had given them, their perfume reviving. Agnes felt her depression falling away from her. Polly was walking almost without a limp. Life was good again because Tracey was dead and many people were relieved of worry. It was as if a cancerous growth had been cut out.

Back in her room, she gave Polly her breakfast biscuits, and then went down to the dining room. Her own waitress came up to the table, her face white and her eyes as big and round as saucers. She couldn't wait to tell her news.

185

'An awful thing happened on the hill last night, Mrs Turner, did you know? Have you heard about it, it was on the radio early?'

Agnes had to show interest, horror, disbelief, and make it look real.

'What happened, Maria, not another murder?'

The girl proceeded to tell her – she had managed to get quite a mass of detail. Agnes tried to look interested and gave a few answers and asked a few questions about something she already knew. It was boring and almost brought back her depression. Soon there would be Thelma to cope with, she thought.

Agnes walked up the hill towards the Ryman house. She walked slowly, her head lowered, thinking. She had not wanted to come. She had tried to talk herself out of it by imagining there must be others of the family she didn't know about; aunts, uncles, cousins, members who would be much closer. Admittedly Thelma had never mentioned anyone other than the mother who had owned and given them the house: but that didn't mean there was no one who would come in these very tragic circumstances and offer support. But, according to Jeremy who had telephoned her this morning, the family were not close, never had been, and he had gone on almost pleadingly – 'You get on so well with Ma, do go and help her.' He had been telephoning from Paris and had used the probably truthful excuse that he didn't have the money to make the journey to the Isle of Wight, so he could not possibly come, but that he would be thinking of Ma. He did not mention Richard and rang off sounding more than a little emotional. This had made Agnes decide to go and see Thelma, let her cry on her shoulder.

Even so, she approached the front door with a feeling of apprehension. After all, she had seen everything and more that her friend was going to describe to her. The blood, flowing, then the girl's fall on to the ground dead – the

186

mother had at least been spared that. Agnes pressed the doorbell and wondered who, which one – Richard or Thelma – would answer it. In a way she would prefer it to be Richard – she did not feel so close to him. She wondered, too, how he would feel about the knowledge that had died with his daughter. Relief – surely not, but at least the fear of her ever telling about his secret affair was no longer there. She was gone and silenced for ever.

Thelma opened the door and Agnes was really shocked by her appearance. She looked ill and so much older. Agnes could understand why she had not bothered with make-up – it was only, after all, the second morning away from Tracey's death. Saturday night she had died and today was Monday. Agnes could hardly believe so little time had passed. It seemed much longer since she had left the body and walked away down the hill and back to the Manor Hotel. This morning she had got up early, wakened by Jeremy's phone call. Afterwards she had walked Polly. They had driven up to the downs where the turf was smooth and springy and clean – good for Polly's injured foot. She had managed to run about and enjoy herself just as she used to before that dead horror had taken her and starved her almost to death.

Thelma did not remark on Polly's absence. Agnes realized that she would still think that the little dog was missing, or, in her present state of stress, would not think of her at all. Agnes preferred this. She did not want to talk about Polly with Tracey's mother after what her daughter had done to her. Thelma did not know the depths her dear Tracey had sunk to before she died. Maybe she never would. Did it matter if the plaster saint remained unbroken and perfect in her mother's mind?

'Oh, I'm so glad to see you, Agnes; it's so nice of you to come. It's all been so awful. Richard has been wonderful, really wonderful; he had to go and talk to the coroner. I just could not have done any of it, Agnes, I truly couldn't. If you'd seen her, she looked so awful, all that blood. I thought she'd been stabbed – you know, like that other

poor man, but she hadn't. She was bleeding from somewhere – I don't know where. I don't understand any of it.'

Agnes let Thelma babble on, sometimes not making
much sense. She told Agnes how she had gone into
Tracey's room, then found her outside, in the lightning and
the rain and the thunder. How she was dressed – that
seemed to have been a terrible part of the shock, her
clothes, and she went on about the butterfly on her right
shoulder. The fact that she didn't even know about the
butterfly seemed to be so very important.

'I told Richard it must have hurt her, you know, the
needle and putting the colours in. And she never told me
about it – her mother, Agnes, never even mentioned she
was having it done!'

It went on and on. Agnes was longing to leave: she was
not a person who enjoyed sharing emotions. She sat opposite Thelma and could not bring herself to go and put an
arm round her friend. She had always been the same, even
when dealing with bereaved patients – a hand on the arm,
a brief touch was always the most she could manage.
Thelma was dry-eyed as if she had cried all her tears away,
but she kept putting both hands up and covering her face,
then lowering them and clasping them together, the grip so
tight that the knuckles gleamed white. She stood up.

'I'll go and make us some coffee, Agnes.'

She took no notice of Agnes's raised hand waving away
the idea of coffee. She smiled a wintry smile and made for
the kitchen. Agnes said no more and didn't try to stop her.
Perhaps the mundane task of making coffee and drinking
it would do her good in her present state of turmoil and
grief. She sat, looking out into the garden, thinking about
Jeremy, about Richard and, strangely enough, about the
two poor nuns in London. She couldn't seem to get them
out of her mind.

The sounds of china in the kitchen interrupted her
thoughts and she looked up and tried to smile as Thelma
placed the familiar tray and two steaming cups of coffee
on the table between them. She picked up one cup and

placed it in front of Agnes, picked up her own cup and lifted it to her lips, then put the cup with its contents untouched back in the saucer on the tray.

'I keep feeling she will come back after school, or some-time this evening, grumbling about her mobile, or wanting supper quickly so that she could get up to her room and log on. I can't believe I'll never see her again.'

Agnes tried to make suitable replies. She wished she did not know so much about the girl who had died, how she was dressed, and her clothes stored in that wretched case. Did Thelma know about that? Agnes could mention none of the girl's shortcomings, indeed she had to be very careful before she uttered any remark that might give away more knowledge than she was supposed to have. Polly, too, was a subject with numerous pitfalls. Thelma seemed to have completely forgotten the dog being lost; the stress she was under had put it completely out of her mind. Agnes hoped she would go on forgetting the missing Polly. She tried to turn the conversation a little and ask about other things.

'How is poor Richard, he got on so well with his daughter, didn't he? He must be grieving, Thelma.'

Thelma nodded, closing her eyes as if she had a headache and again covering her face without saying anything for a few minutes. Then:

'He spoiled her, Agnes, she had only to ask for something, however expensive or silly, and he would get it for her. Sometimes he undermined my suggestions. It used to make me cross sometimes, very cross indeed.'

Agnes nodded, then veered away from that. There again danger lay; Agnes was only too aware why Richard spoiled his daughter. What a situation the girl had managed to build up in the space of her short life. How many people would be relieved at the news of her death?

There was silence for a moment as the two sipped their coffee. Agnes was beginning to feel there was very little that could be safely said. The silence was interrupted by the doorbell; shrill and demanding, it pealed twice. Agnes half rose, but her companion was quicker getting to her feet. She was taken completely by surprise, Agnes could see that.

'Whoever can that be, Agnes? I really don't want to see anyone. I suppose I'd better answer it.'

Outside in the hall Agnes heard the front door opening and then a surprised, 'Oh, Denise, it's you. How very kind of you to come. I didn't hear your car, is your father with you?'

There were steps across the pine parquet of the hall floor. The girl that Thelma led into the room was tall, slender and looked much older than Tracey. A pretty but unsmiling face turned to Agnes as she was introduced; her lower lip, thick and sensual, did not curve into a smile but she looked at Agnes with a sulky look of recognition although Agnes could not remember ever meeting her.

'Oh, Mrs Turner, Polly's mistress – no, Daddy isn't outside.'

Her voice was low and full. Agnes let the remark about her dog pass, and Thelma seemed to miss it altogether. She asked, 'How did you get here, Denise, did someone bring you?'

Denise turned away from Agnes and faced Thelma, taking time before she answered, then: 'May I sit down, Mrs Ryman, if you don't mind?'

The remark sounded, and Agnes felt it was intended to sound, rather pointed, as if to show the adult Mrs Ryman that she was not being particularly polite. It had the desired effect.

'Oh, I'm sorry, Denise, please do sit down. Would you like a cup of coffee? I can get you one in a moment?'

'No, I'm all right, thank you. I've left the bike outside the garage. It's Tracey's, was Tracey's. I used it to get here. I rode it from Newport. It's quite a nice ride. Tracey didn't ride it much, I can't think why. She pestered her father enough to get it for her. I remember her telling me about how she had to go on and on at him.'

190

Thelma Ryman looked completely baffled, her white face puckered in sheer bewilderment.

'But Tracey didn't have a bike, Richard and I talked about it and decided against her having one. Are you telling me he gave in and got her one in the end? She never told me.'

Denise shrugged her shoulders and thrust out that heavily lipsticked, sensual lower lip again. 'Well you know your daughter, Mrs Ryman, if she really wanted something, she'd get it, no matter how. Your Richard hadn't much chance to refuse, had he?'

Thelma turned to Agnes; she looked very ill. Denise slumped back in the chair, watching both adults, her eyes calculating.

'What does she mean – *Richard hadn't much chance*. Do you know what she means, Agnes? What is going on? Things seem to be happening all round me that I know absolutely nothing about. It's a horrible feeling.'

Denise's cheeks went quite pink. She looked as if she knew she was treading on dangerous ground and had maybe said more than was wise, or than she had intended. Suddenly she seemed much younger than her sixteen years and much more vulnerable. She looked down, her hair falling forward and hiding her face.

'Perhaps I shouldn't have said that, Mrs Ryman. It just slipped out before I thought – and I shouldn't have called him Richard but she always did.'

She stuck out one long, slim leg and Agnes noticed that her denim jeans were trimmed with rhinestones round the ankles. Her hair was permed and had obviously frizzed in the rain. She kept pushing it back behind her ears but it fell forward almost at once, half hiding her face. Fingernails painted pearl white were long and square, but the polish was chipped on some of them.

Thelma seemed to be galvanized into new life, and her voice was stronger: 'Well, tell me, Denise, you started this, why did my husband not have much chance? Come along, I want to know.'

'Tracey caught him with his secretary in bed. It was when you went to see your mother who was ill, and she held it over him like a lot of other things she got to know about, about him and his . . . his ways.'

Thelma Ryman almost smiled; her look was contemptuous, not at all dismayed.

'I knew all about that, Denise. When it happened he didn't tell me, but he is no good at telling lies. He's a weak man and I make allowances for that. When you get married you will probably have to do the same.'

Denise seemed relieved at the cool way her gaffe had been taken. Agnes, too, was surprised. The girl hadn't been dead two days and she was being discussed as if grief at her death had already evaporated. Was that what she deserved, Agnes wondered? She thought of Polly and her heart hardened. The nuns, Jeremy, so many people had hated and feared the girl. Well, she was gone. Tracey was no more.

Agnes got up, the appearance of Denise had made her nervous, jumpy. She felt in a way reassured that Denise knew little or she was sure she would have blurted it out. She prepared to leave, but Denise took on a purposeful air and something in her manner made Agnes change her mind. This was not the time to leave. She sat down again and fixed her eyes on Denise. The girl did not speak for a few seconds. Her hands gripping the arms of the chair showed white knuckles as if her pretended calmness was not a true reflection of her inner feelings. This tension radiated itself to Thelma, who got up, her movements jerky. She looked as if she could, for the moment, stand no more of the girl's revelations although she had dismissed the first one with such contempt.

'I will go and make more coffee, Agnes.'

She ignored Denise's refusal and left the room. Agnes spoke to the girl, her manner severe and also dismissive.

'Don't tell me anything, Denise. Wait till Mrs Ryman comes back. That surely is the correct thing to do.'

They waited in silence. Denise sat with her hands

clasped in her lap, her eyelids lowered. Agnes was surprised at Denise's appearance. For some reason she had visualized a rather short, dowdy person, downtrodden by her friend Tracey's more dominating personality; a girl, although older by two years, following the younger girl's lead in every way. But Denise was taller than Tracey had been, with a slender, attractive figure. Her hair, frizzy and blonde, suited her. Like so many youngsters, she constantly put up a finger and moved the strand of hair away and just as constantly, it fell back and the movement was repeated. No clip or slide seemed to be used to keep the hair back in place away from the eyes. It was the fashion, Agnes supposed, and Agnes found it irritating.

Quite suddenly, through the window, out of the corner of her eye Agnes saw Thelma cross the side of the garden that led to the garage. She did not see her return but in a couple of moments, Thelma came from the kitchen with the tray of three cups of coffee. She placed the tray on the usual coffee table and cast a look at Denise of such malevolence that Agnes was surprised the girl did not see it, but she was looking with some distaste at the coffee which Thelma had lifted from the tray and put, cup, saucer and silver spoon, in front of her. Thelma was moving very deliberately. She placed the new cup of coffee in front of Agnes and stirred her own cup, just as deliberately, and then she turned to Denise.

'Well, Denise, what more have you got to tell me?'

Agnes was amazed at Thelma's response and her self-control. She waited for Denise to speak, her eyes fixed unwaveringly on the girl, her mouth set in a line so that her lips had almost disappeared. Denise picked up the silver spoon and stirred her coffee. Agnes noticed that the girl's hand trembled.

'Well, come along, Denise. I want to know everything, all the things you and Tracey got up to, plotted, indulged in without my knowing.'

Denise remained silent, frowning as if she did not know

how to begin, then she replaced the spoon in the saucer, not having touched the coffee, and began.

'It was Douglas, my boyfriend, that's why it all started. He and I had been going together for two years. I really loved Douglas – we were an item. I dreamed about marrying him one day, having babies, even though he was an addict – he was on methadone, but he couldn't or wouldn't kick the heroin. Then when Tracey moved down to the Island and into school, she started a play for Douglas. She was too young for him but that didn't make any difference. She was after Douglas – made a friend of me, too. Any rave on a Saturday, she was there; any party, any booze up. Dressed up, made up, she looked more than fourteen. I warned Douglas, but it was no use – anyway, she could get heroin, crack, E, uppers, downers – anything.'

'But where? Where could she get all those things? She hated drugs and people who took them. She told me some of the pupils at school smoked cannabis but she wouldn't have anything to do with –'

'Where did she get them, indeed, Mrs Ryman? I soon found out what was going on at a party. Tracey had met a couple of medical students – they were both users. That's when she learned about blackmailing.'

At Thelma's little wail of protest, the girl turned to her, shrugging her shoulders.

'It's no use, Mrs Ryman, that's how your Tracey was.'

Denise seemed to have lost her inhibitions now. Tracey had left behind such a tangled web of lies and deceit. As the story progressed, Agnes began to feel a very profound relief. Nothing had been said about the night of the murder, nothing about Polly's abduction. Nothing about Jeremy's lifestyle. Agnes was quick to realize that the more tasty and remunerative blackmailing had to be kept secret and those involved, like Agnes, Jeremy, Denise and goodness knows how many other victims who could be relied upon to give out more and more money, must be treated with discretion and kept, as it were, on the back burner.

Warmed at will and used until useless. Agnes breathed a little prayer of thankfulness that Tracey had been silenced, snatched away before much of what she knew could be used. A terrible way to obtain her silence, but Agnes, thinking of Polly's suffering and misery, Jeremy, Richard – those poor silly nuns, and Denise too, probably, could not be sorry for the girl's fate.

Denise stopped talking and sipped the cold coffee. Not, Agnes suspected, because she wanted it, but because she was embarrassed – but not at all remorseful over what she had had to tell. Thelma looked across at Agnes, then again put both hands up and covered her face. She was not crying, just, Agnes felt, shutting out the light. After a few minutes she dropped her hands into her lap and turned again to Denise.

'Tell me about the butterfly, Denise, the butterfly on Tracey's shoulder.'

'Oh, the tattoo, we both had one done, just for a giggle. We didn't tell anyone. My father would have gone ballistic if he had known I had a butterfly done.' Denise looked questioningly at Agnes, as if to say 'For goodness' sake, why is she asking about that?'

'I saw it on her shoulder in the police lights. It was rather pretty, really. I thought how strange she never told me she was having it done. It wouldn't have hurt her too much, would it, Denise? I would have gone with her if she had wanted me to. I wouldn't have minded her having it done if only she had asked me.'

Somehow the reference to the butterfly destroyed Denise's composure. She broke into a storm of weeping. It was as if the mention of the butterfly and Tracey's mother's acceptance of it broke her.

'I'll probably go to prison, Mrs Ryman. Tracey got me busted. She gave me the bike and in the pocket, where the spanners and puncture things are kept, she put her bag of drugs – heroin, uppers, downers, some cocaine. I've got to go to court, then probably to prison. I told the police the bike wasn't mine but they didn't believe me.'

195

Through her sobs she had more to tell and worse.

'She had sex with my Douglas, not because she was fond of him but so that she could blackmail him. Sex with a fourteen-year-old girl: he was on the hook.'

'But how could this Douglas do such a thing to Tracey? My daughter was little more than a child.'

'Do it to her – how could *she* do it to Douglas? Little more than a child maybe, Mrs Ryman, but a very evil and scheming child, believe me.'

'But you were there, Denise, you could have stopped her, warned Douglas of the crime he was committing, not let Tracey use the drugs, not sell them. You must have taught her all she knew, she spent so much time with you, staying in your house. Surely both your parents must have had some idea how she was behaving, stealing out of her own home, dressing in those awful clothes – someone must have guessed?'

Denise shook her head, pressing a crumpled tissue to her eyes, rocking backwards and forwards in her chair, showing the frustration she felt: Thelma wouldn't accept the fact that she had given birth to a clever, manipulative, devious child and was now blaming someone else, her friend, for what Tracey had developed into. So many parents, Denise thought, don't know their own children, what they were doing when they were away from them, who they were with, how many rules they were breaking. Tracey had been so clever, particularly where her mother was concerned. To her she was the perfect daughter – how well and cleverly she had been deceived. Tracey could have reached any height she wanted, her scholastic prowess was real, she could learn with ease. And yet she had ended up dead, presumably from a dose of some drug which she herself sold to her juniors, companions and what she called friends.

Thelma suddenly stood up. She looked as if she could stand no more.

'Please go, Denise. I don't quite know if I should be pleased you came and told me all these dreadful things about my daughter. I suppose eventually I would have been told – found out about all this. I really don't know.'

Denise got up. She looked at Thelma through red and tear-filled eyes. She could hardly speak. Agnes watched her make the usual gesture, putting up a finger and pushing the fair strand of frizzy hair back behind her ear; it fell back over her eye immediately. She made for the door of the sitting room. Agnes had a fleeting feeling of pity for her – after all, the girl might face a prison sentence that could ruin the rest of her life. She would have a record to live with.

Denise was almost at the door, when suddenly Thelma called her back, her voice loud and determined.

'Oh, Denise, please take the bike. I don't want it here. I didn't know my daughter had one and I would rather not even think about it being here.'

Denise looked across at Agnes, who had hardly spoken. Even now she did not make any sign that she had feelings on the matter. The girl shrugged her shoulders, wiped her eyes again.

'Very well, Mrs Ryman, if that's what you want.'

She left the room, followed by Thelma, who walked closely behind her until she reached the front door, then she stopped and let the girl walk round to the garage where she had left the bike. Thelma stood for a moment, watching, until Denise disappeared round the corner to the garage. With a strange look on her face, she rejoined Agnes in the sitting room. She gathered up the three still full cups of coffee, put them on the tray to take back to the kitchen.

'I think I feel like a drink, Agnes. Brandy and ginger ale for you? I feel rather shattered somehow.'

Agnes had risen to her feet, intending to leave. 'I thought you might like to be alone now, Thelma?'

Thelma shook her head, made a dismissive gesture. 'No, no, Agnes, please don't go for just a moment.'

Agnes sat down again. She felt so relieved that the

killing of the hotel porter hadn't even been mentioned. Polly, the leather coat – none of it even touched on and the one who knew all about these things could no longer speak.

A bird sang in the garden. From the kitchen came the clinking of glass. Then another, louder noise, a scream, a clatter, the sound of a bus or car on the main road stopping, brakes slammed on, tyres screeching. Agnes remembered seeing Thelma crossing the garden towards the garage where Denise had left the bike. What had she done? Had Denise taken the little side road down to the main road? Yes, she would have, it was the quickest way back to the Newport road.

Agnes felt slightly sick. Perhaps nothing had been done to the bike, that path, beloved by Polly, was always sticky and slippery even in dry weather. Anyway, it was nothing to do with her. She began to look forward to her brandy and ginger ale, a drink worthy of a small celebration, she thought, and smiled a little.

Thelma came in with the two glasses, pale, pale amber. She looked white, but composed, as if she had just wakened and was not quite orientated to new surroundings. Agnes looked at her curiously, and took a glass from her hand.

'I thought I heard something outside, Thelma, a sort of crash – something on the road, perhaps. Did you?'

Thelma took a sip of her drink and shook her head.

'No, I didn't hear anything, Agnes, but then the road gets busy at this time in the morning and we can just hear the traffic going to and fro.' She took a deeper drink, her eyes brimming over with tears. 'I keep thinking Tracey will come in through that door, but she won't ever again. All those things she did, nothing I knew about, though so many people knew that were not close to her at all. I was her mother and I knew nothing. I thought she was the perfect child. How could I have ever been so foolish, so tricked by someone I loved so much – too much, perhaps, to register her faults?'

Agnes did not attempt to answer her. These questions could only be answered by two people: a mother alive and suffering, the other dead. She finished her drink and got up ready to leave.

'I must go now, Thelma, and this afternoon I shall return home. I will come back if you want me to.'

Thelma looked up at her, frowning as if she was trying to think ahead, make herself see the future.

'I would like you to come back for Tracey's funeral, Agnes – after all, she didn't do anything wrong to you, thank goodness, did she?'

Agnes was silent for a moment before she answered, then she straightened her shoulders a little and half closed her eyes, thought of Polly with her injured foot waiting.

'No, Thelma, she didn't do anything wrong to me.'

She raised her hand and walked steadily to the front door, away from the house, away from the shadow of that evil girl, and felt as she left the holds the girl had had on her fall away. Many other people, she knew, would be feeling the same. It had been an experience and given her something to think about for weeks to come.

Her goodbyes at the Manor Hotel were friendly; everyone had a special goodbye for Polly, who, except for a slight limp, was almost her old self again. The receptionist, and Agnes's own little breakfast waitress, all expressed their hope that Agnes and Polly would come back for another visit soon. Agnes said she would come back for the funeral of the young girl on the hill, whom they had all heard about, but hardly knew. In a way she was slightly sad to drive away from the hotel where so much had happened. With Polly beside her in the passenger seat where she loved to be, she gave one last wave and drove off. Back to Amy and boredom? She wasn't sure, but anyway, there would be the animals she longed to see again, the cats, the big wolfhound, the Major, the hedgehogs, the goat. How many more were there? How many fewer? Had Amy taken in any new animals, had the kittens found new homes? She had been so taken up with her own problems, not to speak of Polly's problems. So much had gone on that there had been little time or opportunity to have long talks with Amy on the telephone. One last piece of news had been given her by the friendly receptionist as she left.

'Oh, what do you think, Mrs Turner, a girl on a bike had an accident. She must have come down that awful little lane that ends up on the main road, lots of traffic there. That hill seems fated, doesn't it? She is seriously injured, I believe.'

Agnes had answered with assumed surprise. 'Oh, really? Yes indeed, that hill does seem fated.'

Denise, she thought, and was it really an accident? She shrugged away thoughts of the happenings in the Isle of Wight and continued on towards the car ferry.

Chapter Nineteen

Agnes drove carefully on to the ferry, carefully because there was a little hump to negotiate as you drove on to the ramp up to the ship's deck. She did not want to disturb Polly, who was on the passenger seat beside her, sitting up now and again to look around her, but at the moment curled up in the sunshine and appearing to be asleep. She seemed almost recovered now from her imprisonment and cruel treatment. Only her paw with the missing claw seemed to give her a tiny bit of trouble and she occasionally licked it vigorously. The Isle of Wight vet had discharged her, telling Agnes that he could not do any more for the little dog; the claw had been pulled out and would probably not grow back because the nail bed had been destroyed when she had been fighting so hard to get out of her prison.

Agnes felt she had been away for months. She had come for a quiet, restful change – in some ways to get away from Amy. But the change had been anything but restful or quiet, and she had the feeling she would be rather pleased to see Amy's familiar figure, and listen to her usually rather trite little tales about what had been going on while she had been away from the mainland. Parked in the place indicated, Agnes broke all the rules this time and remained in the car with Polly. Dogs were not allowed in the restaurant, and Agnes had absolutely no intention of leaving her. She got round the problem quite easily by smiling pleasantly at the yellow-coated official and undoing her seat belt, giving him the totally false impression that she was going to leave the car. He had smiled back at Agnes and continued on his way down the line of cars and not looked in her direction again.

The sun glistened on the cars. Agnes opened her windows. Polly sat up and licked her foot. The picture of Tracey, blood pouring from her mouth and nose, brought no feeling of pity. Tracey died by her own hand, killed by the drugs she had swallowed to give her a lift, a 'buzz', without any thought for the harm she was causing herself or others. Well, she had got the final 'buzz' and was no more. Agnes stroked Polly gently on the head. The little dog responded as she always did, rolling on to her back and expecting a game, which Agnes couldn't give her in the car. She promised a short 'walkie' when they had left the busy part of the town and reached a more suitable place.

As when she had lived on the Island, Agnes was conscious of a quickening of everything as she drove off the ferry. The traffic seemed to be more congested and faster, even the pedestrians seemed to be moving more rapidly. Would the slower pace of the Island suit her better nowadays? She couldn't be sure.

Amy greeted her as if she had been away for years. She was full of things to tell Agnes about the behaviour and adventures of the animals she had been left to look after. Tippy, her black cat, strolled behind her as she walked back down the garden path, helping to carry Agnes's luggage. Amy was obviously bursting to tell Agnes about all the exciting things that had happened while she had been away. Mostly tales about the animals, Agnes suspected; small, trivial but comfortable tales. She longed to hear them. Wilma the wolfhound came slowly across the room. She was an old dog and had trouble with arthritic limbs.

'She had toothache badly after you left. I nearly telephoned you about it, Agnes, but then I thought you had gone away for a break, for a holiday, a change from dealing with animals, so I took her to the vet and he took the tooth out under anaesthetic. I was worried she would die, but she didn't. A lot of pus came out from under the tooth. She was better almost at once – what a relief it was, Agnes!'

A long story about Harry, the more active hedgehog, leaving home and returning to his little enclosure two days later took more time. Then, over a cup of tea, Amy suddenly realized she had done so much talking she hadn't given Agnes time to speak. She had to finish the tale of Harry the hedgehog:

'So, he found his way back, Agnes, all by himself. Wasn't that a wonderful thing, and he managed to scramble over the wood you put there.'

Agnes agreed and gave full marks to Harry. At last Amy got around to asking Agnes about her time away, whether she felt better and rested, what had Brighstone Manor been like, and was the food good? The questions came out in a rush as Amy asked them without, Agnes felt, a great deal of interest in her answers.

Yes, the rest had done her good. She felt much better. Yes, the hotel was very good and she had been very well treated, and yes, the food had been first class. Yes, she had a most interesting time and, one way and another, she had made a few new friends and acquaintances, but nothing much to them really. No one outstanding, but then they were only a bunch of humans, weren't they?

Amy smiled as Tippy jumped up on her lap.

'Not as clever as hedgehogs, eh, Agnes?'

Agnes smiled and twisted her teacup in its saucer.

'No, Amy, not nearly as clever as hedgehogs.'

Epilogue

Gradually the sharp memories of all that had happened at Brighstone faded for Agnes. Polly completely recovered, even her missing claw space seemed to fill in and she no longer licked the foot or held it up, 'old soldier' fashion, for Agnes to stroke and sympathize.

Thinking it over, Agnes decided that when Tracey's body was released for burial and the mystery of what drug had caused the sudden terrific loss of blood was solved, no matter what Thelma Ryman said, she would not go to the funeral. A cheque arrived from Jeremy Ryman for the amount she had lent him – a note enclosed saying that he had sold two pictures and thanking her again for lending him the money. He also added as a postscript that he was not coming back to England for his sister's funeral. He hoped Agnes did not think he was cold, but he felt, he said, absolutely no sorrow at Tracey's death. Agnes could quite understand this.

Only one thought haunted Agnes. She wished she had been able to kill Tracey, to run the knife into her as she had into the would-be rapist. This would have been a just reprisal, she thought, for the treatment the girl had subjected Polly to. Anyway, it was over now. Thelma, Richard, Jeremy and the dead Tracey – not a family she felt she wanted to remember.

'Did you make any new friends there?' Amy had asked her with little real curiosity.

Agnes had shaken her head positively.

'No, nobody I ever want to see again,' she answered. 'They were all rather expendable.'